HIS LOST LOVE

MANHATTAN BILLIONAIRES

AVA RYAN

1

LIAM

"LIAM." Michael Jamison, one of my closest buddies since we met at freshman orientation at NYU fourteen years ago, blocks the door, preventing me from entering his new apartment in downtown Manhattan. His scowl suggests that I've come strapped with explosives and begun waving the detonation button in his face. "What the hell are you doing here?"

I shrug and try to look harmless as I pass him the nice bottle of wine I brought as a gift.

"Unless I'm mistaken, you're throwing your little housewarming tonight."

I gesture over his shoulder, where a sizable crowd has assembled and appears to be happily enjoying cocktails and jazzy music against the panoramic backdrop of the Hudson River with the Jersey skyline in the distance. He and another college friend of ours, Jake Quinn, recently went public with the medical device company I started a few years back. I should mention that I got a degree in chemical and biomedical engineering before I went to Harvard Med and became a cardiac surgeon. Hey. I'm brilliant, ambitious and talented. Don't expect me to apologize for it. Anyway, I won't bore you with the details, but I invented a couple of devices that make cardiac procedures a hell of a lot easier. Michael and Jake were my early investors. I combined money I inherited on my father's death together with their money. Which means that we've all experienced a significant uptick in our bottom line this year, although I still practice because that's my first love. Now we all try to out-apartment and out-car each other. And I plan to start dabbling more in the real estate market when a good opportunity presents itself.

"I thought I'd check the place out," I continue. "You know I'm interested in real estate."

"Cut the bullshit," he says, his scowl deepening as he snatches the bottle. "You're here because you want to see my sister."

I arrange my expression into something that hope-fully suggests that the idea never crossed my mind.

"I just want to catch the view you've been bragging about." I crane my neck, trying to see past his big head, but there's no sign of her. Mia, his twin, was also in our class at NYU, by the way. "Looks nice. Your apartment could almost be a boat that sits directly on the water. Not as nice as *my* view, though. You letting me in?"

"No. I've been walking a tightrope ever since the two of you imploded back when we graduated. You think it's easy for me to be Switzerland all the time when the two of you have avoided each other for years? Now she's going to think that I set this whole thing up so you could ambush her."

"Yeah, well, now I'm back in town." I moved back last year during my mother's final illness. Now that I've settled her estate, it's time for me to settle things with Mia. "It's past time for Mia and me to stop avoiding each other. We're fully grown adults now. Not hotheaded kids. The city should be big enough for both of us."

"Couldn't agree more. Why don't you text her and see if she wants to grab coffee or drinks like a normal person?"

"Because I'm here now." The part I don't mention? That I've worked up the courage to show up tonight and doubt I'll be able to produce any new courage if I leave without seeing her and then need to text her. I decide to drop the act. "Is she here?"

"She's here," he says grimly.

I feel a tremendous surge of adrenaline. And something that feels strangely like triumph.

"What's it going to be?" I ask.

"Fine." He jerks the door all the way open and lets me pass. "Just make sure she knows that this was *your* idea. I didn't want you here, and you know it."

"That's not strictly true," I say, now scanning the room for any sign of her. "You said you were having your housewarming tonight. You also said that Mia would be here. I took that as a warm invitation to enjoy your hospitality."

"Huh. Funny. Because I'm positive I stated it as a dire warning for you to stay away."

"Semantics," I say, then catch sight of Jake, who materializes out of the crowd with a scotch and soda for my benefit. I receive it with a grateful one-handed hug and a pointed look in Michael's direction. "Finally. A *true* friend."

"Fuck you," Michael says mildly.

"Saw you coming," Jake tells me as I take an appreciative sip to shore up my nerves. "What'd I miss?"

"Liam's here to see Mia," Michael supplies with his usual stir-the-pot enthusiasm and wicked glee at someone else's discomfort.

"Fuck *you*," I tell him, then spy her across the room and experience a sudden catastrophic system failure that freezes me to the spot. Seriously. It's a wonder I don't choke on my tongue.

These two, naturally, notice immediately.

"You planning to grow a pair and talk to her?" Jake asks me, not bothering to hide his sudden obnoxious smirk. "Or are you going to stand here picking your nose all night?"

"I'm betting on the latter," Michael says. "Knowing Liam like I do. Based on long and painful history. Speaking of history, what was that Julius Caesar quote? We talked about it in ancient history freshman year."

"What, *I came, I saw, I conquered*?" Jake says.

"That's the one." Michael claps me on the back with his free hand and gives my shoulders a squeeze that makes me want to see how many of his gleaming teeth I can knock out with a single punch. "I'm thinking Liam's quote would be *I came, I saw, I froze*."

"Either that or *I came, I saw, I shat the bed*."

With that, my two so-called best friends launch into a round of raucous laughter at my expense. Not that I don't deserve it at this point in the evening, when my ongoing paralysis acts as an embarrassment to me and probably my entire family for two or three generations back. Still, I wonder what it is about these two idiots that has made me keep them around this whole time. Probably the threat of blackmail for all the dumb shit they witnessed me do.

I unstick myself with tremendous effort and peel my eyes away from her long enough to glare at these two. Mia Jamison and I are ancient history. This doesn't have to be a whole big thing. There's no reason why the two of us can't exchange a quick greeting and break the ice after all this time. Clarification: no reason except that a) she's so engrossed in a conversation with some woman that she doesn't know I'm here yet; and b) I'm still trying to grow that pair of balls I'll need to make the long walk across the room to say hello to her.

"Maybe if I had better wingmen, I'd be over there by now," I say bitterly, gesturing to a passing server for a refill on my scotch and soda. "How about you help a guy out rather than kicking him when he's down?"

"Look," Michael says, his amusement vanishing. He slings that arm around my shoulder again, reeling me in for a few urgent words of advice. "You're building this up in your mind. She's still just Mia. The same girl you met on our study abroad in Rome."

That's exactly what I'm afraid of.

Luckily, the server returns with my drink just then. I snatch it off his tray, and down the entire thing in a couple of rough gulps.

"*Go.*" Michael relieves me of my empty glass and jerks his head in her direction. "Say hi. Get it over with. It's getting harder the longer you stand here. You're thirty-four fucking years old. You know how to talk to a woman."

That's true. But there are standard human women. And then there's Mia Jamison.

Separate categories.

"You're right," I say grimly, more because I'm sick of myself than from any sudden infusion of courage. "I need you two to keep eyes on the situation for me. Be on standby. Keep the car running. Maybe get a fire extinguisher. Just in case."

We all laugh.

"Get outta here," Jake says. "Report back."

"You got it."

"And if you hurt my sister again? I'll kill you," Michael adds with a hard glint of bloody murder in his eyes.

I take off without disputing his assertion about who did the hurting in my relationship with Mia. My feet get heavier as I work my way through the crowd, which is elegant and nicely liquored by now. By the time I get within ten feet of her, they weigh a ton apiece. My steps slow. My heart races. And all I can do is stare, because there she is after all this time and I can't fucking believe it.

Mia Nova Jamison.

My first love. The woman whose image, smile and laugh burrowed their way into my brain one Roman summer when I was twenty and have remained there ever since. Resisting all my best efforts to eradicate them.

Like malaria or the kudzu that suffocates trees in the South.

I'm not happy about my excitement here, mind you. Why? Because I hate Mia Jamison for the way she left my life and for the condition she left me in when she did it. I should mention that up front. And I'm not talking about your garden-variety hate, as in *I hate sushi. Let's get pizza instead*. I'm talking about the kind of hate that gets stronger over time, rotting you from the inside out.

Sometimes it simmers. Sometimes it boils. Either way, the hate has no problem whatsoever existing alongside my ongoing fascination with this one woman.

Even so, my lingering hard feelings don't stop me from staring at her. And I doubt they'll ever stop me from wanting her.

You can't blame me for that. She's got a Liv Tyler vibe that's enough to make people lightheaded when they see her. But her hair is blacker, her skin paler and her eyes bluer. Her dimpled smile is all her own, as radiant as a Tahitian sunrise. She's always been lean and athletic. That hasn't changed if the way her strappy and slinky black dress pours over her thighs is any indication. With a dress like that, you start to wonder about the panty situation. If any. She wears a pair of killer heels that really work for her, but not as well as they work for me and my impressionable dick.

She laughs at something the woman says. The husky sound combines with the flash of her white teeth and the confident way she flips her hair over her bare shoulder to form something glorious. I can't lie about it. She's on top of the world tonight, clearly. I allow myself to be mesmerized and wallow in that smile for several suspended seconds.

I'm allowed. I haven't seen it for twelve years.

But then, without warning, she turns her head in my direction as though she's heard my heart thundering over all the ambient noise. No surprise there. The two of us were always great at creating our own energy field. Our gazes connect across the ten feet that separate us. I feel that connection as a zap of electricity shoots straight up my spine. She stiffens, her eyes widening. Her smile fades, leaving something stricken behind as color floods her face. She recovers quickly, peeling her attention away from me and recapturing most of her social graces for the benefit of her friend, but she's not that good an actress.

Except for the part when she acted like she gave a rat's ass about me back when we were in college.

That was good.

This? The unmistakable flare of panic in her big baby blues? The glitch in her composure as she smooths her hair with a hand that now looks a little shaky? She's rattled and she can't hide it. I consider that a win. God knows she's done nothing but rattle me since the day I laid eyes on her.

In a stroke of good luck, I complete my approach just as the woman excuses herself from Mia, leaving Mia to hesitate before squaring her shoulders and turning to face me. Maybe she was tempted to take off with the woman, but the Mia I thought I knew would never do that. She's many things—merciless witch comes to mind —but a coward isn't one of them.

Sure enough, she hitches up her chin, eyes glittering.

"Liam Wilder. I wasn't expecting to see you here."

I shrug and slide my hands in my pockets, buying myself time to get my shit together. It's not easy to think straight while being in her presence and hearing the throaty sound of her voice again.

"I'm full of surprises."

"That you are. I didn't know that Michael had invited you."

"He didn't, but I'm sure that was an oversight." I ease closer, arrested by the subtle defiance in her expression and by her scent, some carnal blend of flowers that defies description and is exactly the way I remember it. "You probably didn't know I was back in town."

"Odd, huh? You'd think a news flash like that would make the front page of the *Times*."

I laugh. I can't help it. One of the most intriguing things about Mia has always been the way she sharpens her tongue and wields it like a samurai sword, slicing and dicing people like a professional.

"Actually, Michael did mention you were back in the city." She hesitates. "And that your mother had died. Sorry to hear that. I'm sure it wasn't easy."

"Thanks," I say, which is all I can manage when I think about my mother's decline and death. She wasn't a gem in the mother department, but she was the only parent I had left, given my father's sudden cardiac arrest death right before I started college. Not to mention the fact that Mia seems concerned for me, and a tender emotion from Mia is, sadly, like a hit of heroin to a recovering addict.

I am evidently the addict in question. No recovery here, boy.

"Did dying make her any nicer?"

"Nope," I say with a startled laugh. "It'll take more than a visit from the Grim Reaper to soften my mother up."

She starts to smile with me, then catches herself and stops.

"You look great, by the way," I blurt.

One of those delicate brows goes up.

"I pay a personal trainer, a hairstylist and an aesthetician to keep me spackled together these days. Glad to know I'm not wasting my money. And you're not trying to flirt with me, are you?"

"Would it work?"

"Absolutely. Just like me going outside right now and trying to swim across the river to Jersey would work."

I laugh again, somehow resisting the growing urge to swallow her whole. She's *that* delicious.

"You looked great before all that, as I recall. Matter of fact, back in the day, I'd be looking forward to the end of the night and figuring out what you've got on under that dress." I pause to give her a once-over that lingers on her small breasts, curious to see if the attention is enough to make her nipples bead the way they used to. Ah. There it is. So that hasn't changed. Thrilling. "And you'd be looking forward to letting me."

Those luscious lips curl into a crooked smile without a trace of humor in it.

"Twenty-year-olds aren't known for their smarts. Back in the day, I survived on frozen pizza, donuts, diet soda and five hours of sleep most nights."

"Don't expect me to apologize for the sleep deprivation," I say, sweet memories making my voice husky. "We had better things to do in bed, as I vividly recall."

The bright patches of color in her cheeks intensify.

"Maybe, but I'm trying to stay away from stupid now that I'm older. If there's nothing else? I want to mingle with the people I actually want to see. Have a great night."

She turns to go, but I'm not done here. Not by a long shot. Not when being in Mia's presence again makes me feel this buzzed and *alive*. I don't know what I've been doing with my life this whole time, but it wasn't *this*. And *this* is something I need a lot more of.

"I understand you're designing for one of the big houses these days," I say quickly, before she can take off.

I try to recall which one it was, but my overstimulated brain can't call up the information at the moment. Ralph Lauren, maybe. "I'm impressed."

She makes a derisive sound. "Sure you are."

"I'm dead serious," I say, feeling a surge of the hate again, along with the sour taste of bile in the back of my mouth. "I know *exactly* how much your career in fashion means to you. Although I could have sworn you said you wanted to design wedding dresses. Or am I remembering that wrong?"

I realize my arrow hit home by the way she stiffens.

"Oh, so *that's* why you're here." She says it with the grim triumph of Sherlock Holmes when he slides that last clue into place and discovers who the murderer is. "Career advice."

Wrong. I want to remind her that I still exist. That while *she* may be living her Oprah-sanctioned best life, some of us aren't so lucky. That she still has her nasty claw marks all over my life.

"Well, that's why you ran off to Milan after graduation, right? To learn to make wedding dresses? So you could start your own atelier one day?"

"There was no *running away* involved," she says, the thinning of her lips belying her sweet tone and evident determination not to let me ruffle her feathers. "I got an apprenticeship in Milan and moved there."

"What about your dream of making wedding dresses?"

"Not all dreams go the distance," she says, her expression stony now. "But since you're so curious, you should know that I periodically make custom dresses for people through word of mouth. Matter of fact, I have a wedding this weekend."

I know that already, but now is not the time to mention it. Not when she's raised such an interesting topic.

"Any other dreams in particular?"

"Not at all," she says smoothly.

"Glad to hear it, Starlight," I say, adding a nice layer of mockery to my voice because I know it will infuriate her. And because I want to punish her for acting like the two of us didn't have joint dreams that died an ugly death. "I'm glad you have everything you ever wanted. And that there are no lingering hard feelings. No need for things to be awkward between old friends."

"We're not *old friends*." She can barely get the last two words out. For one thrilling second, I wonder if she actually wants to take a swing at me. I find my ongoing ability to push her buttons fascinating, I must say. "And don't call me *Starlight*."

"Why not? Nova is still your middle name, right? It means *star*, doesn't it?" I keep my voice silky. "Starlight is a perfectly good nickname even if you're not *my* star anymore. Why change things up at this late date? You're free to call me by *my* nickname if you want."

"*Asshole*? You don't mind me using that to your face?"

"No," I say with a startled laugh. "Brad Pitt."

"I'll pass on that. If there's nothing else…?"

She takes another step away, eager to leave me.

I hastily catch her warm arm and press my thumb to the thumping pulse in her wrist, twice as eager to keep her here. The reaction is instantaneous. Her eyes widen. Heat flares between us, exactly the way you get a whoosh of a flame when you light a gas grill.

"Are you here with someone?" I ask.

I hate myself for the sudden urgency in my voice,

which reveals my eternal weakness for her. But not as much as I hate her for bringing it out in me when I've done my best—for *years* I've done my best—to hide it if I can't overcome it.

"My personal life hasn't been any of your business for years, Liam," she says. "As you know."

She manages a lot of vehemence, but I'm fixated on the flickering heat between us. And the way she doesn't pull away. My gaze drops to her dewy lips. My mouth actually waters, which is what happens when you're dying for a taste of something.

I have a tough time hoisting my attention back to her glittering eyes, but I manage eventually.

"I'm not so sure about that. Have a drink with me. Let's see where the night takes us."

That does it.

"There's no *us*," she says, finally pulling free and using that same hand to give my cheek a sharp and condescending pat. "I know there's no other woman in the world like me, but I'm sure there are several here who'd be happy to hook up with you tonight if you twinkle those hazel eyes at them."

"What if I twinkle them at *you*? Will that work?"

Crooked smile from Mia. She takes a step back toward me. Eases closer. Tips her chin up as though she wants to kiss me. *I* ease closer and dip my head, planning to let her.

"Poor Liam. You need to understand that I would go back to my studio, find a needle and thread and sew my pussy shut before I *ever* gave you the pleasure again."

I bark out a laugh, riveted by this woman who surely knows that nothing makes my blood race like a challenge.

"We'll see about that. *Starlight*."

She looks murderous as she pivots and stalks off in those killer heels, giving me the distinct pleasure of watching her hips and ass work in perfect synchronicity as she goes.

2
MIA

"WHAT ARE you doing way down here at the bar by yourself?" comes a male voice a few minutes later, startling me out of my whirring thoughts. "This is a cocktail party. You're supposed to mingle."

It's Eric Carson. Handsome and auburn-haired, he's a work colleague, one of my best friends and my plus-one for tonight. On the one hand, I don't appreciate the interruption when I'm trying to get my shit together here. On the other hand, I'm going to need some help getting myself off this dangerous ledge where I suddenly find myself. God knows I'm not going to talk myself down.

"I just need a minute," I say, accepting a flute of champagne from the bartender with a grateful smile. "I need to catch my breath."

He gets a closer look at me and frowns, taking my elbow to steer me way down to the end of the bar. "You okay? You look funny. Like you've seen a ghost."

"That's exactly how I feel," I say darkly.

His expression clears. "I get it," he says, nodding

sagely. "You saw the ex. What's his name? Liam? You mentioned you heard he was back in town. You look freaked out."

"I am not *freaked out*," I say. That's right. I'm a horrible person who has no qualms about lying to a good friend's face.

"Ah. So there's some other reason why you look so hot and bothered."

"I don't look *hot and bothered*."

Let's just say he seems less than convinced, which doesn't help my foul mood. Thankfully, he doesn't call me on it.

"So how'd it go?"

"Wasn't good," I mutter, then disappear behind a healthy few swallows of champagne. "But I'll be fine."

Oh, how I wish that were true.

I decide that now is not the time to mention what a jolt to my system it was to see Liam Wilder staring at me again after all these years. For one thing, he's insanely gorgeous with his Viking vibe going on. Tall. Blond. He's got all the muscles, shoulders and physical presence anyone could ever want or need. His piercing hazel eyes always possessed the unholy talent of reading exactly what *I* want and need. Physically and emotionally.

Imagine being young and naïve enough to give your heart to the first guy who gives you an orgasm. Imagine thinking that you've met your soul mate at the age of twenty. Now imagine the heartache when you realize that the guy couldn't be trusted to water your plants while you're on vacation for a week, much less to hold your heart in his clumsy hands. Now quadruple that heartache and you'll have some small idea of how hurt I was when my relationship with Liam blew up in my face.

On second thought, cancel that. Multiply that heartache by ten and you'll have some idea how foolish I feel right now upon realizing that, despite the distance of all these years and despite all those painful lessons learned, I'm still attracted to him. Still intrigued by him.

"Where is he?" Eric asks.

I take a discreet glance around, but there's no sign of Liam in the crowd. I order myself to be relieved rather than disappointed by his renewed absence.

"I don't see him."

"So no lingering feelings? You'll be fine if you see him somewhere with a date?"

I open my mouth to say something breezy and unconcerned, but sudden immobility strikes at the thought of Liam showing up at, for example, Lincoln Center Jazz with someone beautiful and accomplished on his arm. I'm not kidding you when I say that the mere idea makes me want to find a baseball bat and start smashing things with it. Which is ridiculous, because Liam is not the sort of man who'd spend twelve years—or even ten minutes, frankly—pining after a lost love. You'll have to trust me on that. I'm sure that Liam has been through dozens (hundreds?) of women since the two of us were together.

But I never had to see him with them. That's the thing. And I don't want to start now.

"Liam Wilder is a free agent. I couldn't care less where he slings his dick these days."

Eric narrows his eyes and considers me closely. "I'm *almost* convinced."

"Oh my God," I say, my heart sinking. "I'm totally screwed, aren't I?"

"You'll be okay," he says, surprising me with a bracing kiss on the cheek. "You'll get it figured out."

"From your lips to God's—" I say, breaking off when a tall man materializes at my side, looming.

It's Liam, I realize with dismay and an unwelcome shiver of excitement.

"Hope this guy isn't bothering you, Starlight," he says, his flinty and speculative gaze swinging between me and Eric.

My simmering temper notches a little higher. I'm not sure how many more times this jackass is going to interrupt my evening, but I'm close to my limit. The unabashed amusement from Eric as his brows shoot up and he mouths *Starlight?* at me don't help matters.

Worse, Liam is *right* there. Right at my hip, where I can smell that amazing scent, some clean combination of linen, soap and warm skin. My entire body seizes up with the rightness and simultaneous wrongness of standing there like this. A thousand lifetimes ago, it would have been the most natural thing in the world to ease closer to him. If I had, he wouldn't have hesitated to sling a possessive arm around me.

"I told you not to call me *Starlight*," I tell Liam, who looks supremely unconcerned by my ire as he sips his drink with one hand and slides his free hand into his pocket. "Second, it'll be a cold day in hell before I need *your* help to handle a man who may or may not be bothering me."

"Sorry. Liam Wilder," Liam says, withdrawing that hand again and extending it to Eric. "Guess I can't count on Mia to make the introductions. She's always been rude like that."

"I have *not*—" I begin hotly.

"Eric Carson," Eric says, shaking hands with Liam and working hard to smother his startled laughter.

"Pleasure," Liam tells him. "So are you and Mia…?" He points back and forth between me and Eric in the universal gesture that could mean anything from "hooking up" to "married."

"My personal life is *none of your business,*" I tell Liam, my outrage growing exponentially by the second. "Anything that ever happened between us is ancient history. Don't forget that."

"Mia and I are *not,*" Eric tells him, neatly deflecting the laser strikes from my eyes. He seems charmed by Liam, which is galling but no surprise. Most people are. "My fiancé would take a dim view of me getting too close with a woman a couple of months before our wedding. He's jealous like that."

"Best wishes," Liam says, now beaming as though Christmas has come early.

"Appreciate that. And speaking of my fiancé, I'd better give him a call and check in. Be back in a few."

With that, Eric takes off, leaving me alone and vulnerable. The traitor.

"Now we can have a drink," Liam says, sliding onto a barstool and patting the empty one next to it before signaling to the bartender. "More champagne for Mia. I'll have a scotch and soda."

"I'm *not* having a drink with you," I snarl.

"Fine. You stand near that empty barstool and sip your drink while staring straight ahead. I'll do the same. Just make sure you don't accidentally turn your head in my direction."

I hesitate, torn between my desire to never give this man an inch and my annoying urge to prolong this interlude with him and see what happens. My intimate lady parts, which have always felt as though they are

humming with electricity in his presence, vote enthusias-
tically for the latter.

"*Sit*, Mia Nova," he says quietly, patting that empty
stool again as his smirk slowly recedes. "We're ancient
history. You said so yourself. What could happen?"

There's one thing I should mention.

Liam Wilder, in addition to being a ridiculously
handsome Viking god in need of a ship, has soulful eyes.
The kind of eyes that pull you in deep and keep you
there even though *there* is a dangerous place where
sharks circle and one drop of emotional blood in the
water will lead to a feeding frenzy and your swift obliter-
ation. The kind of eyes that stare into all your dark
corners and don't flinch at what they see. The kind of
eyes that block out everything else in the world.

Some sort of semi-hypnotic state takes me over, and
I sit.

I suppose that was always a foregone conclusion.

The bartender returns with our drinks, giving me the
excuse I need to look away while I try to regain my
composure. Actually, *regain* is probably the wrong word,
since I never have composure in Liam's presence to begin
with. I need to run off, steal someone else's composure
and return it at the end of the night, when I'm safe from
Liam.

"What should we toast to?" he says, raising his glass.

I clear my throat and grab my own drink. "The
Nets?" I ask sweetly.

We both love basketball and spent many fun hours
shit-talking each other because he loves the Heat and I
love the Nets.

He scowls. "To new beginnings," he says, then clinks
and sips.

"Whatever you say," I say, then also sip, determined to get this over with as quickly as possible.

"By the way, I decided it's best that you never started your own atelier."

Much as I'd like to ignore it, the subtle taunt in his voice scrapes right over my raw nerves.

"Excuse me?"

"I mean…wedding dresses? *You?*" His stare is direct, unwavering and contains all the warmth of a winter storm blowing the South Pole. "You're not a fan of anything to do with committed relationships. Last I heard."

As if *he's* a fan of committed relationships.

I sit there seething and impotent. I'm a nonviolent person who's never slapped anyone in my life. Tonight is shaping up to be the ideal time to change all that. But then I'd give Liam the satisfaction of knowing he got to me, and I can never allow that.

But I *can* switch this up and push one or two of *his* buttons.

"Well, you know." I swivel my stool around, rest both elbows on the bar and give my back just a hint of an arch as I cross my legs. Enough to emphasize my negligible cleavage. Don't get me wrong. The best thing you could say about my small breasts is that they're perky and occasionally allow me to go braless. Like tonight. Evidently, he notices, if his sudden greedy interest in the outlines of my nipples and bare legs is any indication. "I enjoy sex. The city is filled with handsome men who are happy to enjoy it with me. Some of them are probably here in this room tonight. Why tie myself down to one man?"

His gaze, slow and appreciative, trails down my

body. I'm tall, so the process takes a few beats. By the time his heated attention returns to my eyes, my nipples are a lot harder and I feel the sweet ache of arousal between my thighs. And I'm betting that if I reached for his crotch, I'd discover that my nipples aren't the only hard things around here.

"Say the word," he says in that black-velvet voice. "As a handsome man in the room tonight, I'm happy to help you out."

Funny how tempted I am to let him. The unwanted temptation makes me hate him even more than I normally do.

"No thanks," I say, then take a sip of my drink. "Anything else?"

"Yeah." A muscle pulses in his jaw. "Seriously, though. Congratulations on your success as a designer. I always knew you'd achieve great things."

Those soulful eyes hit me with a steady beam of sincerity that makes me want to cry. Probably because I didn't know that the cost for this success would be quite so high. And because I never imagined that my heart would still feel so empty even after I achieved so much of what I thought it desired.

I have a great job, yeah, but it's not my dream job. I'm hitting my mid-thirties with no husband and no prospects, unless I want to suddenly get much more enthusiastic about online dating. No kids. And a lot of empty nights home alone in the fabulous apartment I bought by myself for myself.

But…he *does* seem to mean it.

Something inside me softens. I don't want it to, but it does.

I open my mouth. Hesitate.

"Congratulations on your success as a doctor. And as an entrepreneur." I read an article about his initial public offering in *Forbes* a few months ago. "I always knew *you'd* achieve great things."

"Thanks," he says gruffly, ducking his head. "That means a lot. Coming from you."

That's one of the more endearing and intriguing things about Liam, not that it cancels out the bad stuff. But he has quiet moments, exactly like this, where he genuinely doesn't seem to understand what an exceptional person he is. My heart, which is seeing way more action than it's seen in the last, oh, decade or so, starts to ache.

If only this guy had shown *this* face a little more often back when we were together. What might have happened? How far could we have gone?

"You're still practicing, though, aren't you?" I ask, arrested. "You always seemed so excited about taking care of people."

"I'll never stop practicing." His voice softens as he looks up and resumes eye contact, jolting something tender inside me that's been dormant for a long time. "If you love something, you can't just let it go."

And that, in a nutshell, is why I need to avoid Liam. At all costs.

He brings too many *if onlys* with him. If only he didn't say things like that. If only he meant them if and when he *did* say them.

And I can't. I just can't.

I hastily gulp down the rest of my champagne. Then I slide down from the stool, wobbling a little in my heels. He grips my upper arm, steadying me, scalding me with

the remembrance of that touch and the way it used to
glide over my body.

"Thanks for the drink," I say crisply, keeping my
gaze lowered as I pull free because I can't risk
connecting with him. Not in any way. Not now, not ever.
"I should find Eric."

"Understood."

I look up again, even though I know better. And
suddenly there we are, staring at each other. Connecting.
Or maybe still connected. Either way, it's bad news for
me. And it's bad news even before I notice the color
rising over his face and concentrating in his cheeks,
giving him a hint of vulnerability that touches something
in the area where my heart used to be.

"I've just been wondering... Did you ever think
about me?"

Did I —?

I could almost laugh at the absurdity of the question.
If only this whole scene wasn't so pathetic. As it is, I
barely manage to silence my strangled sound of disbelief.

Did. I. Ever. Think. About. Him.

It feels unnatural not to tell him the truth, which is
that thoughts of him have tortured me for most of my
adult life. That there were periods when I prayed for
dreams about him, because at least then we'd be together
for a while.

Still, I do my best to keep my expression ruthlessly
neutral, with maybe a hint of bewilderment.

"Why would I think about you?"

He blinks. Then he tenses, the hurt washing over his
expression the way foamy rainbow soap washes over my
car when I get it cleaned.

I turn and start to walk off, determined to get away from him before anything worse happens—

"So that's it?" he calls after me. "We don't see each other for twelve years, we have one drink, you claim you never thought about me and that's it?"

"That's it," I say without breaking stride, congratulating myself on getting in the last word for once.

Until I hear him mutter something behind me.

"Bullshit."

3

MIA

MICHAEL CATCHES me coming out of the powder room a few minutes later. I freshened my makeup and slid my game face back into position, but remedial measures like that don't work on brothers who know you too well to be fooled by cosmetics. And, of course, a fresh layer of lipstick can't quite hide the veiled panic in my eyes.

"You're a mess," he says after taking one look at me.

"You think?" I snap, deciding to focus all my righteous anger on him because *he's* the culprit. My so-called twin brother. I feel as though I've discovered he's a spy for the other side. "What did you expect would happen when you invited Liam fucking Wilder tonight?"

"I didn't invite him." He takes my elbow and steers me over to an alcove in the airy foyer, where there's a bit more privacy. Luckily, the crowd is starting to thin and there's no sign of Liam lurking anywhere. "He showed up because he wanted to see you. And you're not over him at all, are you?"

I suppose I should be grateful I've hidden it as well as I evidently have, but his bewilderment this late in the game only fuels my outrage. I try to scoff but produce only a garbled sound, like a woman in dire need of a lung transplant.

"Of course I'm *over him*. I'm not still hung up on Liam Wilder after all this time. How pathetic do you think I am? I just didn't expect him to show up out of the blue tonight."

My voice contains way more vehemence than is strictly necessary to issue what I'd hoped would be a cool denial.

Naturally, Michael hears it and frowns. "I wasn't expecting this development."

"There's no *development*."

"We'll discuss later."

"Not if I can help it. Anyway, great party. Insane apartment. My friend Eric just left, so I'm on my way out. I'm just going up to grab my purse. I stashed it in one of your many new bedrooms."

"Take the private apartment elevator that leads to the second floor," he says as he comes in for a kiss.

"Stop bragging," I say, rolling my eyes.

I trudge toward the elevator, grateful to hit the end of this endless night. Liam's got me running on fumes and adrenaline, both of which are threatening to fizzle out. Damn him. I'll be doing good to postpone my imminent collapse until I get home to the privacy of my apartment, where my emergency slab of vanilla cake from Magnolia Bakery awaits me in the freezer. Alongside an emergency black-and-white cookie and an emergency slice of Junior's key lime pie cheesecake.

Not that I ever suspected I'd confront an emergency like *this* when I replenished my emotional eating supplies a couple of months ago. My only hope is to limit my consumption to just *one*.

The elevator dings and the doors slide open just as I get mad as hell and decide not to take it anymore. Liam Wilder came back to town. So what? Is that a reason for me to fall apart and stuff myself with empty calories? No, it is not. In a couple of days, we can both disappear into this city of eight million people and never lay eyes on each other again.

At least until Michael's next event. Luckily, Michael doesn't entertain much.

I'm a strong woman. Liam Wilder doesn't get to show up and turn my hard-earned peace upside down. I won't let him.

Just like that, I breathe a little easier.

I square my shoulders, lift my chin and stride into the empty elevator like the confident woman I am. I even start to smile as the doors slide closed and I hit the button—

Until Liam appears with his hands in his pockets and, without the slightest appearance of hurrying, strolls into the elevator at the last possible second. I watch in absolute disbelief as he leans against the brass bar opposite me, crosses his ankles and settles in for the ride, looking as relaxed and unconcerned as a man waiting for the next bus to arrive at his stop.

Except for his eyes. I don't know how any pair of eyes manages to look so hot and so cold at the exact same time. Eyes like that belong to a person who either wants to fuck me or kill me. Maybe both.

In response, my entire body shivers with a renewed current of electricity. Swear to God, it's like I'm only alive when he shows up. The rest of the time? I wait in suspended animation. That's the most galling thing about his sudden reappearance in my life. I thought I'd been living a real life this whole time, but maybe that was all an illusion I sold myself.

"What are you doing?" I say in an alarm-tinged voice.

"That seems obvious. Going upstairs. Same as you."

"Right, but *why* are you going upstairs?"

Maybe I don't look strung out enough yet, because he pauses to cock one of those heavy brows. The effect? A terrifying level of insolence. A man with *that* look on his face has a point to make and won't stop until he makes it.

"Why all the interest in some guy who's such ancient history that you haven't bothered to think about him this whole time?"

I shift uncomfortably in my heels and toss my hair off my shoulder, my cheeks burning with helpless fury. I have the wild idea of hitting the red button and getting someone to come rescue me, but I'm not in any physical danger. I know that. This kind of danger is so much worse. And what would I say when security came on the line? That I don't like how hot it makes me when my ex-boyfriend looks at me like *that*?

"What are you doing, Liam?"

"Coming upstairs to fuck you, Mia," he says without missing a beat.

I don't know what's more thrilling.

The steadiness of his gaze as he stares me in the face or the silkiness of his voice.

I go absolutely still, startled by his baldness in saying it and by the vehemence of my body's response. Nerve endings tingle to life between my thighs and across my bare arms and legs. My breasts ache.

This involuntary physical reaction, naturally, pisses me off.

"Not that it matters to you, but I don't plan to fuck you now. Or ever again."

Amusement flickers across his expression. "Sure you do."

He's so smug. So infuriating. As though this is all a foregone conclusion. As though he can smell my arousal wafting from my pores like sweat after a tough jog. As though he knows that he's the one man in the world with the right combination of eyes, voice and pheromones to make me stupid and weak.

But *I* know something as well. I know that I still have the power to get inside *his* head. Even after all these years.

So I run my fingers through my hair for the pleasure of hearing his breath catch as I cross over to his side of the elevator. Keep going until I'm well inside his personal space. Grip the rails on either side of his arms, caging him. Maintain eye contact as I lean in and angle my mouth a whisper away from his.

"Why would I do something so self-destructive? When I can go downstairs, right now, and find someone to sleep with without all the emotional damage?"

Crooked smile from Liam just as the elevator glides to a stop and dings. "Because none of them can do it like I can, Starlight. And we both know it."

I stiffen, this bull's-eye hitting me right between the eyes in a kill shot.

But he doesn't need to know that.

"Poor Liam," I say sweetly. "Didn't you hear me when I said *ancient history*?"

His expression sours.

Having produced a wickedly perfect parting line for the second time tonight, I decide to make my exit before either the elevator doors close again or he hits me with a wickedly perfect comeback. I do my best not to hurry even though I feel the steady zap of his piercing gaze between my shoulder blades, propelling me like a cattle prod. Luckily, I don't have far to go and arrive at the closed door of the fourth bedroom just as the elevator doors whoosh shut again. So he's gone. Thank God. I feel a huge wave of relief tempered with disappointment and sexual frustration. I feel oddly deflated. All the emotional turmoil makes my hands shaky as I reach for the knob.

That was a close call. I'll give him that. I'm woman enough to admit that I felt the temptation to take another bite of his forbidden fruit and see if it's as sweet as I remember. But did that arrogant SOB *really* expect me to drop my panties and spread my legs for him all just like *that*? After everything he's done?

I make a derisive sound.

"Not in *this* lifetime, Liam," I say with a surge of triumph. "*Fuck* you."

"That's not very nice, is it?"

Liam's voice, velvety as a puppy's muzzle, comes from behind me. As in, *right* behind me.

Startled—only vampires and cats with lost collars move that silently—I stiffen and start to turn, my twitchy hands eager to smack him away from me and open some space between us. But there's no time for that. He steps closer, bringing the entire front of his body, including an erection notable for both its size and hardness, up against the entire back of my body. Worse, he plants one of his big hands on my torso for a lazy caress that sparks tingles in all the valuable real estate between my breasts and pussy. Worst of all is the way he runs his nose and lips across the tops of my shoulders, audibly inhaling the scent from my skin and causing me to melt from the heat in his.

The effect on me is instantaneous and devastating. I tip my head to one side, giving him access to my neck. Tiny hidden muscles between my thighs begin to ripple and clench. Goosebumps erupt over every inch of my overheated flesh. My hips pump involuntarily, thrusting my ass against that big dick. My knees weaken. So does my resolve to do the right thing and keep the walls up between the two of us.

An insidious little voice starts to wheedle inside my head.

It's been so long. You're older and wiser now, right? It's just sex. Where's the harm?

But another part of me, the stubborn part, refuses to give him the win.

Seething now — Liam's just being Liam, but how dare my own damn body betray me like this? — I do my best to break free. Hey. Better late than never.

"Get your hands off me," I say.

I'd have better luck wriggling free from a pool of quicksand, not least because I don't really *want* to be free. That insidious hand of his slides higher, rubbing my aching nipple before cupping the entire breast and making me moan. I can do a lot of things, but thinking straight when Liam Wilder has his hand on my breast is not one of them. In case there's any doubt, I'm sure the sharp hiss of my breath clears it up for him pronto.

"Forget it. I'm going to make you come until your head explodes, Starlight." His voice is thick now. Rough with a need that sounds as though it matches mine. "Which is what we both want. So are you going to open the door, or should I? Or we could do it right here if you want to brace your hands on the wall for me. Doesn't matter to me."

Wild thoughts race through my mind while I grimace and battle physical need, humiliation and euphoria.

Thank God he's back. Thank God he's not giving up. Thank God he's taking control.

But I can't just surrender without drawing blood. My pride won't allow it.

So I look back over my shoulder at him, catching a glimpse of the hard glitter in his eyes.

"I never thought I could hate you worse than I did back then. I was wrong."

To my absolute outrage, he laughs. *Laughs*.

"You think I care? You think you hate me any worse than I hate myself for still wanting you after the way you ripped my guts out? Get real."

With that, he lets me go and opens the door with a hand that's a lot steadier than mine. Then he grabs my wrist, yanks me in after him and slams the door shut.

Part of me wants to dispute who did the gut-ripping in this relationship, but there's no time for that in this arrested moment when our harsh breathing is the only sound in the universe. The glittering skyline on the other side of the endless windows provide just enough ambient illumination for me to see the hard planes of his face and the wild light in his eyes. He looks older now, obviously, with hints of crow's-feet fanning out from the corners of his eyes. He feels bigger, the reedy boy he was back then having given way to this powerful man. He seems harder. Unforgiving. I don't know this current Liam at all. God knows exactly who or what he's been doing since I saw him last.

Despite all that, everything about this scene feels familiar and inevitable.

And I loved him once. *Loved* him with every ounce of blood in my naïve soul.

"Liam," I say, my voice cracking as I reach for him.

We come together hard and fast, our mutual frenzy making it more of a bruising grapple than an embrace as he backs me against the nearest wall. Doesn't matter. He pulls my hair in his eagerness to hold my head in place as his lips cover mine and his tongue sweeps home. Doesn't matter. He leaves no room for space, air or thoughts between us, and that doesn't matter either.

All that matters is that this is *Liam* and he's here with me again. His fresh linen scent is the same. His hot skin is the same. The rough silk of his hair as I fist it in my hands is the same, and so is the taste of scotch in his mouth. His urgent but incoherent whispers and his heavy handprints over every part of my body—breasts, hips, ass, thighs—are exactly the same.

If anyone else manhandled me like this, I'd laugh, throw him out of my bed and finish myself off with my favorite vibrator. With Liam? I can't get hot enough or shimmy out of my damp panties fast enough.

He knows it, too, damn him.

"This is ancient history?" I get a glimpse of the unmistakable glimmer of satisfaction in his eyes before he yanks down the stretchy bodice of my dress and licks each of my nipples. This, naturally, elicits another round of helpless mewling from me. I rake my nails over his back, wishing there'd been time to get rid of his jacket and all his other clothes, then reach for his belt when he

straightens again. He bats my hands away and takes care of it himself, leaving me to work on the zipper. "You expect me to believe that bullshit? That you never thought about me?"

I cannot let him get away with this galling arrogance. "Sometimes I think about the poison ivy rash I had when I was thirteen. That doesn't mean I want it back in my life."

He flashes a smile that's full of wicked intent and bitterness but no humor as he reaches into his back pocket for his wallet, pulls out a foil wrapper and tosses the wallet aside.

"I don't give a shit what you want, Starlight. I'm back. Deal with it."

"This is a one-off," I say, watching him with rising impatience as he tears the wrapper open with his teeth and sheathes himself. At this rate? I'm coming in the next thirty seconds whether he's inside me or not. "You know that, don't you?"

"We're still not out of each other's systems. *That's* what I know."

There's no time for me to digest this grim truth before he yanks the bottom of my dress up, guides me to wrap a thigh around his waist and bends just enough to get the angle right. Then he takes that big dick and slides it home between my thighs, making my world wobble on its axis.

Just a little bit.

We cry out and stare into each other's faces for one arrested second. He looks exactly the way I feel, which is shocked. Shocked to realize that, yes, I've actually allowed things to spiral out of control to the point that I'm letting this man I hate do me up against a wall.

Shocked to discover that he still feels this exquisite inside me. Shocked to learn that the witch's brew of emotions inside me includes this wild euphoria.

"You'll be thinking about tonight for the rest of your life," he says, and there's no mistaking the steely edge of confidence and resolve in his voice as he plants his hands on the wall on both sides of my head. Meanwhile, I wrap my arms around his neck and help myself to handfuls of his wiry hair, bracing myself. "I promise you that."

"Big words," I say, even though I don't doubt him. Not for a second.

"Keep talking," he says before giving my lower lip a quick nip. "I'm just going to fuck you harder."

He's as good as his word when he starts pumping.

In a world where men are happy to sext you about their intimate knowledge of the Kama Sutra and follow it up with a dick pic, as though any of that proves a damn thing, Liam Wilder is still the real deal. His thrusts are deep, sharp and fast, exquisite enough to bring tears to my eyes. They're also so relentless when it comes to hitting my sweet spot and generating electrical pulses that I cry out. Every. Single. Time. There's no shutting me up. Trust me, I try. I know he'll throw this in my face later, but what can I do? It's like a law of physics. You can't shake a bottle of champagne and then expect it not to explode. Things just don't work that way.

I let my eyes roll closed and give myself over to the thrill of his groin grinding against mine, grateful he's got his face pressed to my neck and therefore can't see the way I smile and, yes, shout for him. Nor do I give him any *yesses* or *oh, God, Liams*. Small victories, admittedly, but I'll take any victory I can get. Matter of fact, the way his rhythm falters just as his groans get louder makes *me*

feel as though I've won several Olympic gold medals.
But then the delicious pleasure washes over me in a wave
so enormous that it wipes out everything in my existence
but *this*.

Him.

The way he smells. The way he sounds. The way he
feels. The way he *tastes*.

The way his voice sounds broken and awed as he
stiffens and calls my name.

He spasms against me, and the aftershocks go on
forever. His *and* mine, ricocheting between us.

I'm tempted to laugh with triumph now that I know I
can still affect him like this, but this is no time for celebration. Not with the realization setting in.

Is *cataclysmic* too big a word to use for something as
commonplace as an orgasm? What about *devastating*? Or
here's a good word — *humbling*.

I'm humbled to realize that I'm still the same when it
comes to Liam Wilder. Still weak. Still profoundly
stupid. I thought I'd moved on in my life. Found some
success. Enjoyed other men. Become a strong and confident woman with only passing pangs of loneliness,
quickly overcome. But it was a lie. All of it. Now I know,
thanks to this wall quickie, that I've been living my life
on mute this whole time. I enjoyed parts of it, sure. But
its full potential wasn't *quite* there no matter how much I
pretended it was.

And now?

My heart seizes up and my throat tightens down.

I don't want to think about it. I can't think about it.

Besides. I've got more pressing issues.

He murmurs something vaguely soothing against my
neck, the brush of his lips sparking additional ripples of

sensation across my cooling skin. He works his way up to my chin, nuzzling. I could die from the gentleness of his touch even though I know it's from gratitude for a great orgasm versus, say, actual tenderness. But if he keeps going, he'll discover the tears on my cheeks and realize that more of me is implicated than just my body.

Obviously, I can't have that.

"Mia —"

"I think we're done here...?" I say, turning away before he can kiss me.

He slowly raises his head.

I arch away from him, forcing him to ease his hold on me and pull out. I feel his loss as a continuous tingle between my legs that I'm sure will be there for days. As if I need a reminder of my ongoing foolishness where he's concerned.

Another reason — I must be up to number four million or so by now — to hate him.

I try to get my spaghetti legs under me, but it's easier said than done. Especially in these heels. I wobble. He helps me stay upright via a firm grip on my upper arm. I pull my arm free. He adjusts himself and hitches his pants up, his face lowered and shadowed as he heads for the bathroom.

He doesn't want to look me in the eye any more than I want to look at him.

I hastily wipe my cheeks, find my panties and adjust my dress. By the time he returns, I'm leaning over the dresser mirror wondering if I should bother reapplying lipstick to my ruined face, which would be the equivalent of rearranging those *Titanic* deck chairs *after* the ship has sunk to the bottom of the ocean. I pretend I don't see him there, but that's the thing about Liam. He's always there, even if it's just in the back of my mind. He persists despite all my best efforts to eradicate him.

He clears his throat. "What now?" he asks quietly.

"Now I go home," I say, putting the lid back on my lipstick with a snap.

"That's it?"

I arrange my expression into something carefully neutral as I turn to face him. "I told you. One and done. That hasn't changed."

We stare at each other across the space of ten feet or so.

The lighting isn't great in here, but several things jump out at me. He looks good as new with his damp hair and clothes back in place, as long as you don't look too hard at his untucked dress shirt. I wonder if it's hiding a stubborn bulge. His face is set and grim. I can barely force myself to look into his eyes. They still see way too much.

"A lot of things *haven't* changed," he says. "You probably noticed just now. Why don't you grab a drink with me somewhere? We need to get some things settled before this weekend."

"This weekend?" Dread skitters up my spine. I can almost hear the crane swing the anvil over my head and lower it into position. "What are you talking about? I designed a dress for a wedding in the Hamptons this weekend. I'll be out there. With any luck, you and I will never lay eyes on each other again."

His features rearrange themselves into *gotcha* position.

"Didn't you know? That's my sister's wedding," he says, eyes gleaming with triumph. "Looks like you're out of luck, Starlight."

4

MIA

AFTER LIAM LEAVES, I cobble my hair and makeup back into some semblance of normalcy and use my app to call for a driver. None of which is easy to do with my frazzled nerves, shaking hands and wobbly legs. Then I hurry downstairs to Michael's first floor, cursing the fact that I have to now make it onto his building's elevator to get to the lobby and praying I can sneak out of here and make it home without any further human interaction. The idea of interacting with more people tonight or doing anything other than drowning my new troubles in a long bath and a couple of glasses of Sauvignon Blanc after I devour that slice of cake does not fill me with glee. So I'm less than thrilled when the elevator doors open and reveal Michael sitting idly on a bench. I scowl at him and began a determined march toward the other elevator doors. With any luck, my driver will be waiting curbside for me by now. But Michael intercepts me.

"Don't even try it," I say, furious. "You're dead to me. *Dead*. I am now an only child."

"What, *again*?"

"Now is not the time for you to get cute with me. Why did you even tell Liam about the party tonight? Why couldn't you have kept your big mouth shut?"

"If it's any consolation, I'm not sure who looks worse, you or Liam. Who left like a bat out of hell a couple of minutes ago and didn't hear me calling him. Shirt wrinked. Dick barely tucked back into his pants, by the look of things."

I wince.

It turns out that when you share a uterus with someone, you become so close that you can say anything to each other. That kind of connection can be a blessing at times and a curse at others. Like right now, when I'd rather keep my tragic foolishness to myself. But there's no point in trying to hide it. Michael would know anyway. He always knows, often with little more than a glance.

"*Michael*. I don't want to talk about—"

"Let's go," he says, taking my arm and leading me over to his vacated bench.

"I don't have time for this now, Michael."

"*Sit.*"

I sit, glumly and with great reluctance.

He signals someone while my thoughts quietly spin out of control. The next thing I know, he passes me two shots of something—I assume it's Patron—and clinks my first glass with his.

"To finishing up unfinished business," he says, then tosses his back.

"I'm not drinking to that," I say, scowling. "To new beginnings and bright futures."

"Whatever you say," he says, watching me down my own shot. "I take it your reunion went well?"

"Screw you."

With that, I make quick work of the other shot.

He waits, one brow cocked, eminently patient. His calming presence is exactly what I need at this moment, which is probably why I keep reinstating him as a sibling even in the face of an unspeakable betrayal like the one he perpetrated tonight.

Besides, he was there from the beginning with Liam and me. He's already up to speed on the situation. And I'm in so far over my head that I'm happy for a ride from any rickety rowboat that happens to pass my way.

"Did you think you should warn me that he *might* be here?"

"I'm not allowed to say his name in your presence," he reminds me. "That's been a rule for over a decade. Besides, I thought you were over him."

So did I, I think grimly.

So.

Did.

I.

"It's fine," I say, waving my hand and deciding to try an offhand approach. Who knows? Maybe it'll work. "I was, ah, surprised to see him. That's all."

He nods, saying nothing.

"I don't know why he couldn't have sent a text saying he's back in town like a normal human being if he wanted to see me."

"Then he wouldn't be Liam. And there'd be fireworks whether he texted you or not."

Well, that's sadly true.

"The wedding I've got this weekend? It's his *sister.*"

"Hmmm."

A new wave of outrage hits me. "Jesus Christ,

Michael. You knew about that, too? And you let me get blindsided *twice*? Whose side are you on?"

"He's my best friend—"

"And I'm your *twin sister*. Does blood count for nothing around here?"

An easy shrug from Michael. "I'm on the side of happy people."

"Well, you won't find any of *that* around here," I say with a bitter laugh.

"Not yet. But there could be. If you work some things out."

"There's nothing to work out," I say, aghast. "You were there. You saw the ugly ending."

"I also saw the happy beginning. And the happy couple of years in between."

"That's all over now. It's been over."

"Good point. I'm sure that's why you were back in bed within an hour of seeing each other tonight."

My cheeks flame hot enough to singe my eyebrows. "There may be some, ah, residual chemistry, but I don't want to see his face again. And now we've got this wedding—"

"So don't go. Simple."

"What?"

"Don't go. The dress is made, right? Hand it to the bride and wish her well. What does she need you for out in the Hamptons? I'm sure someone else can zip it up for her."

"First of all, your knowledge of wedding dresses is appalling," I say, flaring up. "Second, Ella and I are friends now. So I'll be there as an invited guest *and* the designer. Liam Wilder is not going to drive me away. He doesn't get to show up and disrupt everything about my life. I'm sure the estate is big enough for both of us to move comfortably without seeing each other."

Michael gives me that unwavering look of his, a disquieting gleam of amusement in his eyes.

"If you happen to run into him—purely by accident —you should spend some time with him. Catch up."

"And why would I want to do that?" I say, ignoring the unwelcome pang of interest at the thought of spending more time with Liam.

"You tell me. A lot of time has passed. He's changed."

Magic words to my weak female heart. Men like Liam don't *change*. When in the history of life has a bad boy ever truly changed? Never. That's when.

So it's with some dismay that I feel my mouth opening and hear the words coming out.

"And how's that, pray tell?"

"He's all about his career—"

"That's not a change," I say, scoffing. If there was ever one thing that was true about Liam Wilder, it was that his career ambitions were the most important part of his life.

"—and he's more settled. Less drinking. I wouldn't be surprised if he's ready to settle down and have a family."

"I'm sure you're right," I say, giving his knee a conde-scending little pat. "And I'm sure that Jimmy Hoffa, Amelia Earhart and Sasquatch are all living quietly together in a house somewhere upstate. Are we done here? As important as this conversation about Liam Wilder is, I'd love to go home sometime soon."

I hastily stand and smooth my skirt, trying hard to ignore the unwanted pang of longing in my chest and belly at the thought of Liam settling down and starting a family. As if that would ever happen. As if *I* would be part of such a happy domestic scene if it did.

But…

I have a guilty little secret, so I may as well confess it now.

I've kept track of Liam this whole time. I'm not a stalker, per se. I don't follow him on social media, but we have friends in common, so I see and hear things. And I Google him every six months or so, usually late at night when I'm between would-be boyfriends and have had one glass of wine too many. I've noted his career progress and many accomplishments, none of which were a surprise, given how ambitious he's always been. I've seen pictures of some of the women he's dated over the years, all beautiful and accomplished. I'm sure any one of them would happily raise their hand if he called for a volunteer baby mama. One other thing that I've noticed? There haven't been any women to speak of in the last year or more. Not that *that* proves anything other than that he's smart enough to keep his personal life off social media.

Still. I'd be lying if I said I never noticed or wondered about him.

My brother gives me a knowing look, almost as if he can see my ambivalence wafting around me like an aura.

"Think about it," he says, also standing and leaning in to kiss my cheek. "That's all I'm saying."

"You've said more than enough," I say briskly, resuming my determined march toward the elevators. "That's all *I'm* saying."

My driver, who's been circling the block this whole time, poor thing, collects me at the curb. I get in and get settled, grateful for the cooling June air on my cheeks and for a quiet moment to stare blindly out the window and process tonight's events. I'm only dimly aware as the car glides off and merges into the honking traffic.

My thoughts quickly turn to another night. Another ride.

"This seat isn't taken, is it?" comes a man's voice during boarding, startling me as I bend at the waist to stow my backpack beneath the seat in front of me. It's the summer after my sophomore year at NYU, and several dozen of my fellow classmates and I are on our way to Rome for a summer of studying abroad. "Oh, shit. Sorry."

"Hey!"

My attention snags on this ticket-clutching idiot, who thinks it's okay to drop into the aisle seat next to me without waiting for an answer. His blue-jeans-covered ass is currently sitting on top of my precious portfolio. So it takes me a second to snatch said portfolio to safety, make sure my sketches are still okay and look up to see what kind of jackass —

Whoa.

He's got rumpled and curly blond hair beneath his Miami Heat baseball cap. Hazel eyes. Really striking eyes. Imagine a young Brad Pitt. Then throw that away and imagine a hotter young Brad Pitt with hazel eyes. Imagine he smells amazing, like fresh linen and warm skin. Now you're starting to get the idea. Now imagine he's got a hint of Harrison Ford's Han Solo cockiness, with a couple of tattoos (I see several cool designs at a glance) on his bare and muscled arm thrown in, and feel free to swoon with me.

"Is it okay?" he asks anxiously, gesturing at the portfolio.

Add Jon Bon Jovi's husky voice for good measure.

"It's fine," I say, glowering. Which is the best way my twenty-year-old brain can think of to hide my intense visceral reaction to him. "Why don't you watch where you put that ass?"

He grins, unleashing a savage pair of dimples that strikes me as double-dipping into God's genetic blessings. There's no reason why he needs dimples like that on top of everything else.

"Sorry. I usually do."

"So what are you doing here? This seat is supposed to be empty. I already checked with the flight attendant. I don't want to be stuck next to some idiot for eight hours. No offense. I'm sure you're a perfectly nice idiot."

"None taken," he says, laughing. "But I don't want to be stuck next to my former, ah…"

"Girlfriend?" I supply, quickly getting the picture. "Fiancée? Friend with benefits?"

"Fuck buddy. Let's go with that." He shoots a furtive look up the aisle, where, sure enough, the Barbie to this Ken is approaching with her Louis Vuitton carry-on and watching the proceedings with a flinty eye. "Listen. Can I sit here? I promise I won't be any trouble."

I don't believe that. Not for a second. Even given my relative naïveté and current state of bedazzlement, I still possess enough common sense to know that this guy is a walking red flag. He's a handsome and sexy bad-boy player with enough innate charm and sex appeal to get me — and probably all the other women in the rows surrounding this one — pregnant by the time we land in Rome. His presence makes my heart thump, my cheeks burn, my blood sizzle and my nipples and pussy tighten with longing. A smart person would see what she could do about getting him kicked off the plane before takeoff. But I already know, two minutes after encountering this guy, that he and smart cannot peacefully coexist in my life.

"Suit yourself," I said, shrugging. "Just don't get on my nerves."

"Deal," he says.

"And take off that ridiculous hat."

He whips it off with military efficiency and tucks it into his back pocket. "You're not a fan of the Heat?"

"I'm a Nets girl."

"And here I thought you were perfect," he says just as Barbie arrives at our row.

"I thought we were sitting together," she tells him in a nasally and vaguely whiny West Coast accent that's every bit as annoying as you're imagining. "We still need to talk."

"Nope," he says with a decent stab at regret as he makes a show of consulting his ticket. "I'm right here in, ah..."

"Twenty-six-B," I supply sweetly, pointing and covering up where his ticket says 32-C.

"Yep," he says without missing a beat. "This is my seat. Have a great flight, Janet."

Janet frowns and studies the lettering above his seat as though she's in training for a flight attendant job. I have the uneasy feeling that she's going to demand to see his ticket when luck intervenes.

"Do you mind?" barks the guy behind her. "You're holding up the line."

"We'll talk later," she tells the guy next to me, resuming her progress down the aisle.

"Bye," he says.

"Thanks," he tells me with an audible sigh of relief as soon as she disappears. "I owe you. Here."

To my astonishment, he pulls out a flask and offers it to me. "You're kidding, right?" I say.

"It's tequila. The good stuff."

"You're such a cliché," I say with a burst of disbelieving laughter as I push it away. "Look at you. The tattoos. The liquor. The groupie. I'm assuming you left your motorcycle in the parking garage at the airport. The whole bad-boy version of Brad Pitt vibe you're going for. What're you trying to prove?"

He looks startled. Some of his swagger and charm recede just enough for me to get a glimpse of what may be the real guy inside the dazzling package.

"The motorcycle's at home," he tells me, his voice gruffer now. "I got a ride to the airport. And you don't know anything about me."

"Clearly," I say quietly, deciding to back off because I can tell I've hit a nerve.

And because there's suddenly something too intense about the way those hazel eyes level on my face and study me as though I've got things hidden that he needs to find. Thoughtful. Curious. Determined.

I get the feeling he's truly noticing me for the first time.

I get the feeling I'm in way over my head.

"I'm not sure why I helped you," I say, giving him a narrow look, desperate to do something to break this spellbound feeling. "What did you do to her?"

He blinks. Frowns. "Why do you assume I did anything?"

I raise a brow but say nothing.

He stares at me. I stare back, waiting. To my surprise, he opens his mouth and gives me something that seems honest rather than the glib answer I was expecting.

"We've been seeing each other for, like, a month. She started asking about my plans for marriage and children."

"I see," I say gravely. "And you weren't ready to make it tattoo official just yet."

He snorts. "I've already had to cover up a lame tattoo I got last year when I was drunk. Nothing else is going on this body unless I'm positive it'll be there for life."

"You are wise beyond your years."

"Janet will never make that cut. Trust me."

"Why not give her more of a chance? With a voice like that, I'm sure she'll grow on you."

He doesn't seem to appreciate my attempt at humor. "I'm trying to become an engineer here," he says with a new intensity. "Then I'm going to med school when I graduate. Harvard, hopefully."

"How do you find time for a serious major what with the partying and the women?"

"I multitask," he says with an easy shrug. "Plus, I'm smart."

"And humble."

"I want to be a cardiac surgeon. Maybe dabble in real estate for fun. I'm not getting married before that. And I'm never getting married to her."

"Worthy goals," I say, impressed despite myself. Finding smart people at NYU isn't exactly revolutionary. But there's something special about him that resonates with me even if I can't quite identify it. "And here I'd taken you for a romance languages major."

He bursts into laughter, then quickly subdues it. "My, ah, dad. He died a couple of years ago. Cardiac arrest."

"Oh, no. I'm so sorry."

He nods, a sad smile working its way across his face before disappearing. That quiet moment of vulnerability is as sexy to me as everything else about him. It touches me somewhere deep inside, at a place no other guy has ever accessed.

"Why am I telling you all this?"

"Because I'm special," I say, only half joking.

"Yeah," he says, his attention briefly dipping to my mouth. "I'm beginning to think you are special."

"WOW, Liam. She must be really special for you to be out here waiting for her."

The unwelcome female voice jars me out of my thoughts early that Friday afternoon, a couple of days later. I stop my mindless pacing alongside a dozen or so luxury cars on the cobblestoned and circular driveway of the Black family's monster estate (owned by brothers Damon, Griffin and Ryker) out here in the Hamptons and look around to discover my younger half-sister Ella, a.k.a. this weekend's bride (she's marrying Ryker), approaching with a look of bemused pity that sets my teeth on edge. That's the moment when the true gravity of my situation begins to set in.

That's right, folks. I am well and truly screwed. I can't eat. I haven't slept. There's not a thought in my head that doesn't have Mia wrapped all around it. I thought my obsession with her back in college could never get any worse, but you'll have to trust me when I say the following:

This is worse. Because now I'm a fully grown man

who should know better but somehow still can't help himself.

So, yeah, I'm screwed.

Not that I plan to admit it voluntarily, especially to my younger sister, who's got all her romantic shit together and will lock down her happy future tomorrow.

So I work hard on looking bewildered.

"Aren't you getting married tomorrow? I'm surprised you have time to notice me out here getting some fresh air."

"Oh, *fresh air*," she says, one side of her mouth twitching with open amusement. "On a beautiful day like today, at a beautiful home like this, you naturally ignored the beach, the gardens, the tennis courts, the pool and the stables and came out here to get your fresh air. On the driveway."

"The air in the stables isn't that fresh," I point out, keeping one eye on the road for any signs of movement, my cheeks beginning to burn.

"Right. And this has nothing to do with the fact that you overheard me on the phone with Mia minutes ago when she called to make sure she's on the right road to the house and will be here any second."

It takes me a lot of effort not to cringe. Didn't think I'd been that obvious, but whatever.

"I don't eavesdrop on other people's phone calls," I say, still watching the road.

"I hope you appreciate what I've done for you, brother. Asking Mia to make my wedding dress. Not mentioning that you're my brother during all the fittings this whole time. Mia and I were getting to be friends, but you've probably ruined that with all your scheming. I just pray she didn't take a can of black spray paint to my dress in retaliation."

"Don't worry. If Mia decides to get revenge on anyone, it'll be me, not you," I say grimly. "You can trust me on that."

"Why do you say that?"

I fold my arms, cross my ankles, lean against the nearest car and try not to sulk at the mention of this touchiest subject. "Long and painful history."

"I thought you were going to see her the other day and break the news that you'd be here. Break the ice."

"It's broken, all right," I say, thinking of me thrusting hard between Mia's toned thighs, her lush and delicious body wrapped around mine. "It's *really* broken."

"So?" Ella asks brightly. "How'd it go?"

I think of Mia's wild abandon as I fucked her and the way it was immediately replaced by murderous anger the second we finished. I think of the radio silence between us since then. I think of what I wouldn't do to touch her again and, more importantly, to have her smile at me again, which is nothing. I think of the soaring hope I feel to be seeing her again soon, only to have it immediately replaced by abject despair because I'm so stuck in this godforsaken purgatory with her that I can't see any way out.

"Not good," I tell my sister.

"Well, you need to fix it. I'm way out on a limb here for you. Don't let it be for nothing. You've got to get her back."

This, at last, gets my attention off the road. I haven't heard such a ridiculous idea since that insidious little voice in my head told me the other night that fucking Mia again wouldn't hurt anything. I zero in on Ella and all her bright happiness about everybody's romantic future.

"Try to keep up. I don't want her back. I want to forget about her. So if you know a good, I don't know, emotional exterminator, I'd appreciate the referral."

"You don't actually believe that, do you?" she says with a startled laugh. "Your denial level is off the charts."

This assessment does nothing for my plummeting morale.

"Now that we're making a stab at being real siblings, I feel comfortable in telling you to back off. Please and thank you."

"You can't be mean to me on my wedding weekend," she says with a pretty pout.

"*Please* and *thank you*," I say again, louder. "With affection."

"Fine. I'll let it go for now, but don't expect me to—"

There's more, but the sound of an approaching car and the responsive thundering of my heartbeat drown it out. Anticipation freezes me to the spot. I watch the road feeling as though my entire existence is on point. Exactly like a hunting dog that's cornered a fox in some bushes.

A sleek black Porsche SUV glides up the long driveway and comes to a stop with all the other luxury-mobiles. The moonroof glides closed, cutting off Nicki Minaj before she finishes telling us about monsters. The engine cuts off.

I watch and wait for a glimpse of Mia—any glimpse at all—cursing the blackout windows and uncomfortably aware of my avid sibling audience.

The door finally swings open and there she is, the architect of all the highest highs and the lowest lows in my life.

Swear to God, I can't breathe as she swings those long legs around and climbs out of the car. My body is so full of lust and cold fury that there's no room in my lungs for air.

I'm not sure why I keep letting her do this to me, but Jesus, she's a master at it.

She's wearing a long and flowing black sundress that bares gleaming golden skin in all directions—shoulders, cleavage, arms and miles of legs. Strappy flat sandals that reveal pretty feet with virginal pink polish. Does she remember that I have a thing for virginal pink polish? I'd bet a million dollars of my new fortune that she does. Aviator sunglasses cover her eyes and add to her air of mystery. Not a hair out of place.

The overall message as she shuts the door and heads in our direction? She is calm, cool and collected. She is aloof and disdainful. I can come or go from her life and my presence or absence will never matter to her because she will remain untouchable. And no matter how many sleepless nights she causes me, how tightly she wraps me around her little finger or how often she makes me wish I'd never been born, she'll remain, now and forever, slightly out of my reach.

The knowledge makes me seethe.

Until I remember that there's *one* place where I can touch her. Luckily for me, the big old house behind me is full of bedrooms and beds. And I'm nothing if not persuasive when I need to be.

The knowledge cheers me up immediately.

"You made it!" Ella cries with a clap and a hop of excitement before hurrying to intercept Mia with a hug. "I'm so glad to see you."

"You're just glad your wedding dress is here," Mia

says, laughing as she returns the hug. "You're not fooling me for a second."

I watch Mia, riveted.

I'm not trying to be dramatic here, but I would kill or die to have that smile directed at me again. To hug her and laugh with her again, exactly like *that*. I know it's not healthy to tie myself in knots over wanting something —*someone*—and I would stop if I could. I swear I would stop and untangle myself from this hellish existence.

But I can't.

I've never figured out *how*.

"I can be happy to see you *and* the dress," Ella tells her, turning her loose. "Speaking of, please tell me it's in the trunk."

"It's in the trunk."

"Thank God." Taking her hand, Ella leads her over to me. Mia tenses and comes closer with all the enthusiasm of Marie Antoinette making her approach to the guillotine. "Liam says the two of you went to college together? I don't think I mentioned that Liam is my brother."

"You did *not* mention it, no," Mia says. Funny how her dark sunglasses do nothing to hide the scathing look she gives me. "That's the sort of thing I would have remembered."

"Liam's the one who recommended you for my wedding dress," Ella tells her, shooting a fond look in my direction. "And I'm so glad he did."

"You knew I had a sister named Ella, Starlight," I say, noting with great satisfaction the way Mia's cheeks redden at my use of the nickname. I plow ahead, determined to get any further reaction out of her that I can. By whatever means necessary. "We were together for two years. You knew *everything* about me. And I mean *everything*. I call her *Starlight* because her middle name is *Nova*," I add for my wide-eyed sister's benefit. "In case you were wondering. I slip up and call her that sometimes. You don't mind, do you, Mia?"

Mia's pleasant expression hardens behind those sunglasses. She gives me a chilling smile.

"I'm fine with college nicknames if you are, pencil dick," she says smoothly, prompting me and Ella to each smother a startled laugh. "As it happens, I *did* remember that you had a sister named Ella. It just didn't dawn on me that *this* was the Ella in question, since I'd never met her and the two of you have different last names. And she didn't have that telltale scent of sulfur coming from her skin, so I didn't know there was a family connection."

"Well. Now you know," I say, trying to quash another laugh. "You won't mind being here with me all weekend, will you?"

"You won't bother me a bit. I brought plenty of bug spray," she says breezily before turning her attention to my sister. "Should we take your dress in, Ella?"

"Yes, but I hate to miss any fireworks between the two of you," Ella says, also laughing.

"Don't worry," I say, infusing my voice with a liberal dose of silk as I give Mia a lazy once-over. I note, with another dose of satisfaction, the way color rises over her cleavage and neck and concentrates in her cheeks, giving her the sultry look I love. "The one thing you can count on when Mia and I get together is fireworks."

Mia doesn't dignify this with a response, or maybe she's too focused on not lunging for my throat and choking me out. Either way, she turns and heads for the car, her spine stiff. The next thing I know, she produces a giant white garment bag and carefully lays it across my sister's outstretched arms.

"Careful," Mia tells her. "It's heavier than it looks. Why don't I help you?"

"Oh, no, I've got it," Ella says happily. "I just don't want to wrinkle it."

"Don't worry. I've got the steamer in my suitcase," Mia says.

"Okay, good. I'll take this inside. Liam, you help Mia with her bags. And don't forget about the separate dinners tonight. One for the men and one for the women. Seven sharp for both of them."

She hurries off, leaving me alone with Mia and the crackling air between us.

"You look good enough to eat, Mia Nova," I say, heading for her trunk. "Which I plan to do later, by the way. I can't think of anything I'd like better for dessert than the taste of your pussy. Sorry I didn't get around to that the other day."

"*One* and *done*," she says through gritted teeth, putting up one hand to stop me and opening the trunk with the other. "And I've got my suitcase myself, thanks."

"Don't be stubborn," I say, frowning. "I'll take it for you. I don't want you to hurt your back."

"Back off."

I hold my hands up and give her space as she hefts a large suitcase out of her trunk and sets it on the cobblestones. Then I fall into step beside her and put my hands in my pockets as she wheels it toward the front door.

"This should be quite the wedding," I say. "They've already got a giant tent set up out back."

The continued sound of my voice seems to cause her

physical pain, judging by her grimace. Or maybe it's the struggle to roll the suitcase over the cobblestones.

"Indeed."

"Ella is crazy excited. I'm happy for her. I don't know Ryker well, but he seems like a good guy."

"I'm sure he is."

She puts her back into getting the suitcase up the steps leading to the front door, which I swing open for her. Then the house sprawls before us, its massive foyer with halls spinning off in several directions, exactly the sort of place where you'd expect Jennifer Lopez to vacation during the summer. I can almost hear poor Mia's heart sink with a thud when she catches sight of the endless staircase. I try not to laugh as she hastily rearranges her face to hide her dismay. All things considered, it's a wonder she hasn't tried to back over me with her Porsche by now.

Ella, who has by now made it upstairs with her precious dress, leans over the railing and calls down to us.

"Mia, your room is the first one on the right in the east wing," she says, pointing. "Liam, I told you to get that bag for her. I'm so glad you're both here with us this weekend. Love you!"

With that, she disappears down the hallway, leaving me gaping after her for a second or two before I blink myself out of it.

"You sure you don't want me to…?" I ask Mia, gesturing at her suitcase.

"*No.*"

We head for the staircase, where Mia lowers the handle and hitches the suitcase up the first step. Then the second. "Don't let me keep you. I'm sure you've got other people to annoy while you're here this weekend. I can't hog you—"

"Did you hear that just now?" I can't quite keep the wonder out of my voice, nor can I stop my heart from swelling inside my chest. And the moment feels even more special because Mia knows about my painful family history and the way my parents stayed in their rotten marriage until my father's death, despite the fact that he had a parallel family consisting of his mistress and Ella, their love child. Ella and I never had much of a relationship until last year, when my mother got sick and I came back to town and made a point of reaching out to Ella. "My sister said she loves me. I know she didn't really mean it and part of it was for you, but she said it."

"She did mean it."

"*What?*"

Something about the dead certainty in Mia's tone catches me by surprise. I stop and face her on the third step, my heart kicking out twice as many beats per minute as it needs.

"She *did* mean it," she says with apparent reluctance, her expression softening with unmistakable empathy as she balances the suitcase between us on the step. "You and her fiancé are all she ever talked about at her fittings, although I don't think she ever said your name. She always just said *my brother*. She mentioned when you took her to lunch a few times and that you gave her a share of the inheritance from your father even though he didn't mention her in the will. She's glad she has a real brother for the first time in her life. She meant it, Liam."

This news is so profound that I can't begin to process it. The fact that it came from Mia is the juicy cherry on top of a giant sundae that I don't deserve and will never be able to consume.

My mother is dead now. My father is long dead. But my sister loves me, which means that we are officially no longer estranged.

Best of all, Mia's here.

She was always lurking inside me, true. But now she's *here*.

"It feels too good to be true," I say, and I'm no longer sure whether we're talking about my sister or something far more important.

"If someone tells you they love you, you should believe them," she says softly. "Try believing them. For *once*."

Something flares between us, too bright to look at. She turns away first and resumes her climb up the Mount Everest of staircases. I stay behind, watching her for a step or two, and then I can't take it for another second.

Not the yawning ache of loneliness inside me. Not the pride stiffening her spine. Especially not the bewildering abyss between us when we once had so much potential.

"Give me that," I say gruffly, yanking the handle away from her and doing my best to ignore the soft brush of her skin along with her outraged peep. "Throw your back out of whack on someone else's watch."

I stride past her and climb the rest of the way by myself, depositing the suitcase inside the door of her room. She catches up to me on the threshold, her face as sour as a gallon of fresh lemon juice.

"Thanks," she says stiffly. "Even though I was

managing perfectly well by myself and would probably have made it eventually."

I want to laugh. But tears are much closer to the surface.

"Do you ever wonder...?" I start, then immediately regret the impulse. "Forget it."

"What?" she asks warily.

I open my mouth. Hesitate.

"You ever wonder how far we could have flown together if we hadn't messed it up so badly? Because I do." My throat tightens, making the words harder to get out. "*I* do."

I'm watching her closely, so I see the moment her eyes fill with all that infinite sadness. She looks exactly the way I feel.

"Don't say things you don't mean, Liam."

A sudden flare of anger burns aside all other feelings.

"How about you stop telling me what I mean and what I don't mean when I finally get the courage to say it?" I say, my voice rough. "You want to talk about *for once*? Let's try *that*. For *once*."

She hastily turns away, ducks her head and starts to go inside her room, her face shadowed.

But I can't let her go right now. Not yet.

"I'm going to burn you out of my system this weekend or die trying, Mia," I tell her, unmoved by the subtle flare of panic as her eyes widen. "For once and for all. I can't think of a better way to spend this weekend than in bed with you. So you'd better start getting your mind around that. Fair warning."

JUST AVOID HIM, I tell myself as I unpack and get settled in my elegant and spacious room overlooking the ocean. I'm trapped here for the weekend with him, true, but this doesn't have to be a whole big deal. It's a huge mansion. There are plenty of other people here. I don't think it's realistic to expect to not see him at all, because that would be asking for too much from this cruel universe. But come on. It's not as though we'll be glued at the hip. I'll see him here and there, but this time I'll be prepared for the onslaught. He'll make eyes at me and try to get laid again. It's what men do. But as long as I keep my wits about me, this doesn't have to be a disaster. Sure, I had a weak moment and succumbed to his considerable charms the other day, but I can't keep beating myself up about it. I'm human. I make mistakes. The important thing is that I learn from my mistakes. Which I definitely do. And don't make them again. Which I definitely won't.

Even when he makes it harder by hitting me with those soulful looks and sweet words of his.

As if he *really* expects me to believe that he's wondered how far our relationship could have gone if we hadn't messed it up so badly. Please. When did he do all that wondering? When he was screwing the dozens of women I'm sure he's been with since the two of us were together? Or maybe he was thinking about me when he reached out and called me exactly never. Or when he never texted me or reached out on social media. Yeah. I'm sure that's it. And now he's back here expecting me to fall all over him with gratitude for his unexpected return into my life?

Delusional, much?

Don't think about it, girl, I tell myself. *Just avoid him. Avoid even the thought of him. He can't disrupt your life if you don't let him.*

Excellent advice, but much easier said than done. Especially now, when I've cranked my blood pressure several notches higher thinking about his smooth arrogance. He's got me fuming. *Fuming.* Like I want to kick a wall or smash something in this beautiful room. Like I want to crawl out of my own too-tight and too-hot skin.

I need to blow off some steam before the girls' dinner tonight. Try to unwind.

You know what would unwind you? Fucking Liam again.

"Shut up," I tell that sly little voice in my head.

I lean against the dresser, thinking hard. I'm sure a place like this has a huge gym tucked away somewhere, but I worked out when I got up this morning. Walk on the beach? Nah. Don't feel like dealing with the sand. Tour the gardens? Don't feel like that either.

What about the pool?

Yeah, the pool. Great idea.

I can swim a few laps, cool off and clear my head in one fell swoop.

I hit the pool deck five minutes later, now sporting my black one-piece and a sarong. I grab a fluffy white towel from a giant basket as I admire this up-close look at how the other half lives. The place has an infinity pool ringed with lounge chairs and tables featuring red market umbrellas, as one does in case one needs to entertain forty or fifty of one's closest friends. It's got extensive gardens. Guest houses. Tennis courts and God knows what else. And all of it overlooks the bright blue ocean, because of course.

Must be nice.

I'm so busy appreciating the general splendor and congratulating myself on finding a secluded and shady spot away from all the wedding hubbub inside that I don't immediately register a swimmer approaching from the far end of the pool with a powerful stroke.

Without warning, the splashing catapults me back to a scene from that summer in Rome.

It's the middle of the night. Liam and I have snuck out, alone, to the pool not far from our dorm rooms. He dives in first, then swirls his arms in a lazy dog paddle as he watches me with hot eyes.

"You coming in?" he says, his gaze sliding over me and my black bikini.

"Just getting a little more comfortable first," I say, making a production out of untying my top and letting it drop to my feet…

I blink myself back to the present with tremendous effort, gathering dread and unwelcome excitement. Look closer, noting the light-colored hair and sinewy arms. A healthy level of panic kicks in—*oh, shit, that definitely looks like Liam* — and jump-starts my flight response. That overrides everything else.

Forget the pool. I don't have the juice to go another round with him right now. I can't do it.

My only hope is to sneak out before he sees me. Abandoning my lounge chair, my towel and, evidently, all dignity, I pivot and hurry back the way I came. Unfortunately, I only make it a couple of steps before I hear more splashing and a wry male voice behind me.

The male voice.

"Leaving so soon?" Liam asks.

"Not at all," I say, stifling a vicious curse as I continue on my trajectory, grab another towel from the basket, rearrange my features into something that hopefully approaches bland indifference, thanking God for the semi-protection of my sunglasses, and head back to my lounge chair. "Just needed a towel."

"Ah," he says with a pointed look at the towel I'd already left on the lounge chair.

I stifle another vicious curse while the scene unfolds and my dire circumstances become abundantly clear.

First of all, he remains in the pool and rests his elbows on the ledge as he sweeps his goggles over his head and smooths his hair out of his face. As you might imagine, the sight of a wet and bare-chested Liam Wilder, with his honeyed skin and muscular shoulders dotted with water droplets and swirling with beautiful ink, is a glorious thing indeed.

Second, something about the light out here hits his eyes just right, making them into sparkling jewels that put the rest of the view to shame.

Third, said eyes gleam with amusement at my expense. Eyes like *that* belong to a person who gives no mercy and refuses to allow unfortunates, such as myself, a graceful way off the playing field. Eyes like *that* see what you don't want seen, and their owner gives zero fucks about how uncomfortable that makes you.

Fourth—and this is the biggie—I just really want him again. I do. I can't help it. At hormone-soaked moments like this, I can't make myself care that letting him touch me again is exactly as self-destructive as using a cactus as a dildo. Liam Wilder will destroy my intimate lady parts for anyone else. I know he will. Hell, he already has. But none of that matters in the heat of the moment. And I have no real expectation that I'll muster up the self-discipline required to, say, resist his indecent no-holds-barred-sex-weekend proposal and keep his stellar dick away from my orifices for the rest of the weekend.

But I have to try.

"Glad you're sticking around," he says, watching me unfurl both towels and arrange them. "We shouldn't have to divide up the house and the grounds. We can peacefully coexist."

"Absolutely," I say. "Even a mouse and a python can peacefully coexist in a tank when the python's sleeping."

He grins, generating a startling display of dimples, white teeth and boyish mischief.

"No need for me to ask which one of us is the snake in that scenario. Are you coming in?"

I shrug.

"That was the plan, yeah," I say halfheartedly. Probably because this giant pool suddenly doesn't seem big enough for the two of us. We're barely dressed, for one thing. For another, he's got the kind of potent masculinity that could, I don't know, impregnate an unsuspecting woman via the water connection. I can't explain what he does. He just does it.

"By all means," he says with a sweeping gesture and a silky note in his voice. "The water's great."

What did I tell you? No graceful way off the playing field.

I kick off my flip-flops, lamenting my sad lack of cleavage while being grateful that I'm pretty fit and at least had the foresight to get a wax before I came out here. I'm reaching up to untie my sarong, excruciatingly aware of his rapt attention, when a phone buzzes on one of the tables on the other side of the pool, startling us.

"Oh, shit," he says, looking around before launching himself out of the pool. "That's the hospital."

Confession: I don't care about the hospital. I care about the view. So I sit on the edge of my lounge chair and admire it under cover of applying sunscreen.

He hurries off in his navy trunks, water sluicing down his very fine body with every step. He's just muscular enough, strong and sinewy without being bulky. Tight ass. Powerful thighs. Calves toned like a soccer player's. Golden skin dusted with that corn-silk hair.

I watch him towel his head, answer the phone on a distant lounge chair and carry on a conversation I can't hear. I'm so immersed in taking mental pictures to savor during the long and lonely nights in my future, when I'm smart enough to stay the hell away from him and therefore need to rely on battery-powered toys and fantasies if I want any sexual gratification, that it takes me a moment to notice the way he stiffens… The way his expression falls… The way his entire mood seems to collapse as he says a few more curt words, ends the call and heads back this way looking like a kid whose next five birthdays and Christmases have just been canceled.

What the—?

My heart sinks as though all that bad news, whatever it is, belongs to me.

Ridiculous, I know.

But I can't help it. I never could when it came to Liam Wilder.

"The pool's all yours," he says, keeping his head down as he drapes the towel around his shoulders and passes me on the way back inside.

Well, what am I supposed to do here? I stare after him, thinking hard, but there's no real choice to make. Obviously, I'll need to suspend my plans to hate him for all eternity long enough to make sure everything's okay. Reboot the hating after that.

"What's up?" I call after him.

He pauses without turning. "It's nothing," he says, shrugging.

Like I believe that for two seconds.

"Liam," I say when he sets off again.

He swings back around, holding his arms wide in a helpless gesture. I'm dismayed to see the crystalline shimmer of tears and a tremor in his chin.

"My patient died. Fifty-five years old with two kids in college and a husband of thirty years. All of whom are going to be wrecked. She had another heart attack even though we did everything humanly possible to save her. I have a dead patient for no good reason." He nails me with an accusatory look, eyes flashing. "And don't pretend you care."

He's right. In a just and fair universe, I wouldn't care at all if he's upset. I'd be sad about his poor patient, sure, but no one has ever hurt me as badly as he's hurt me. If *he* now feels a little pain, I should take it as a welcome sign that karma is on the job and keep it moving with my own life.

But the universe is not just and fair. And I can no more stand by and watch him suffer than I can grab a straw and drink this pool dry.

"I don't care about you or your feelings, but you can sit for a minute before you go inside," I say. "I'll make sure to hate you twice as much for the rest of the weekend."

That gets him. He cracks an unwilling smile that quickly disappears.

"I'm sure you will," he mutters.

"Sit."

After another slight pause, he sits on the end of my lounge chair, on the other side from me. Close enough for me to feel the force field of heat from his big body. Close enough for me to see the couple of freckles across his nose, the black-and-gold striations hidden among the hazel in his eyes and the bleakness in his expression.

"Tell me," I say.

"I don't know why she died." He can't seem to get the words out fast enough. "I've been doing this for a long time now. I know a lot about hearts. I invented my device because I wanted to do my bit to make sure no one else gets the call that their loved one dropped dead for no good reason."

"Like your father," I say quietly, adding the part he can't bring himself to mention.

He hangs his head and quickly swipes his eyes. "After all this time, I still don't know jack shit about hearts. I don't know." He raises his head and looks at the sky with a shaky laugh. "Maybe I'm in the wrong field. I should've become a proctologist."

I can't help but smile. Same old Liam. Still a perfectionist and a control freak after all these years. That's probably why he's a great cardiac surgeon.

"Or maybe you're not God," I say. "Maybe you've saved as many people as you could, but some hearts can't be fixed. It doesn't matter how much skill or training you have or how hard you work at it. Some hearts are too far gone and there's nothing you can do."

By the time I get to the end of my last sentence, it dawns on me that I may not be talking about his patients. I may be talking about something else altogether. Something that snuck into the conversation when my defenses were down and I couldn't guard against it.

For a fleeting second or two, I entertain the false hope that maybe he's too upset to notice. I tell myself to look away. Not to let him see. But if there's one thing about Liam, it's that he notices everything about me. Even the hidden things.

Especially the hidden things.

Which is probably why he's looking at me like that. Direct. Unwavering.

"That's the thing about cardiac surgeons, Mia," he says quietly. "We try to fix hearts."

"Like I said," I say, forcing myself to look away at last, now that all the damage has been done. "Some hearts can't be fixed."

"Maybe. But you never know until you try, do you?"

I stare at the beach, determined not to look at him again. Not now. Not with this lump in my throat.

"You're the expert."

"I've got to go call the family," he says.

"Yep. You should do that."

But he doesn't go anywhere. He sits there, staring at my profile, the heat of his attention a thousand times hotter than the sun's heat on my bare shoulders.

"You should try not being so special all the time, Mia Nova." I hear a tinge of tenderness in his voice. It calls to me. Touches me. "Maybe then I wouldn't still be thinking about you after all these years. And I'd leave you alone in peace."

"I'm not special," I say with a shaky laugh as I risk a glance at him. "You haven't figured it out yet because you're not that smart sometimes."

He blinks, shuttering away something that I would have liked to investigate further. Something bright. Hopeful. I get the terrible feeling that I've just stamped on spring's first tulip for no good reason. I also get the terrible feeling that maybe *I'm* the one who's not that smart in this scenario.

"Yeah, okay," he says tiredly, turning to go again. "Whatever you say."

He starts to lever himself up, making the towel shift away from his chest. That's when I notice it for the first time.

"Hang on," I say sharply, grabbing his wrist and keeping him right where he is. "What's that?"

"What?"

"That *tattoo*," I say, pointing to his chest. To his left pec, right over his heart.

To the tattoo he didn't have when we were together.

It's a beautiful image, as though the artist married the radiant points of a compass star with the rays and body of the sun. It's glorious.

And I may not be that smart sometimes, but I know starlight when I see it.

He stares at me and waits, saying nothing as color rises up his face and settles over his cheekbones.

"When did you get that?" I ask, too stunned to think about hiding the urgency in my voice.

The longest pause of my life passes.

"The day before we broke up," he says.

Everything inside me clenches. With pain. With loss.

I put all that aside to think about later, after I get the answer to my second question.

"Why haven't you covered it up by now?"

Another pause. Longer this time.

"I wanted to." He swallows hard, making his Adam's apple bob. He clears his throat. But he doesn't look away. "I couldn't."

His bombshell thus lobbed, he turns and walks off, leaving me alone with my spinning thoughts.

7

LIAM

THE MEN'S evening consists of dinner at a ritzy steak-house and an early arrival back at the house for cigars and single-malt scotch in the library, although part of the group breaks off to play pool in the game room. Not a stripper in sight, which is fine by me. At our age, most of us have had our fill of partying and strippers. I know *I* have. The only naked breasts I want in my life tonight belong to Mia. Since that's not looking good at the moment (the women are still out at their bachelorette dinner) and since I've generated all the small talk I can for now and need to pace myself if I hope to get through the rest of the weekend with these relative strangers (the Black brothers seem like nice enough guys, but I'm not in the market for any new best friends, and I feel like they're only keeping me around to be polite, because my sister is the only one I know here), the thing I really want to do is make a quick escape upstairs. Lounge in my room. Decompress for a while and get my mind right for the ceremony tomorrow.

"I'm heading upstairs, folks," I say when we hit the

foyer, trying to infuse my tone with the appropriate amount of regret. "Check in on a couple of my patients and check my emails. Thanks again for a great din—"

"Hate to tell you this, Ryker, but your future brother-in-law sucks," interjects the middle brother, Griffin, before I can finish. From what I can gather, he's the one I need to keep my eye on. He's got a biting comment for everything. It's not hard to imagine him taking a sharp left turn into outright assholery at the slightest provocation. "He barely said a word at dinner. Now he won't even smoke a cigar with us. You sure you want to marry into this lame family?"

"Yeah, I'm sure," Ryker says happily. The groom-to-be says everything happily these days, as far as I can tell. I never met him before he hooked up with my sister, so I have no basis for comparison, but I can only imagine that he's in imminent danger of making his entire head collapse into his neck if he keeps splitting his mouth open and grinning like that. This much delight can't be normal, even for an enthusiastic groom. "He's not the member of the family I'll be in bed with every night for the rest of my life."

"Fair point," Griffin says, eyeballing me with open amusement. "I'm guessing it's no real loss if he goes up to bed early anyway. A guy like this probably doesn't even know how to light a cigar. Waste of a good Cuban."

I think back to my partying days and have to laugh at this older and wiser version of me, whose fondest wish isn't to party but to have a moment alone with his thoughts.

"I smoked my fair share back in the day," I say.

"Of…?" Griffin asks.

"Everything."

A murmur of new respect ripples amongst the brothers, who elbow each other.

"We have a player," Griffin says. "Who knew?"

"Have a drink with us," says Damon, the oldest brother, gesturing toward the library. "Won't take that long. What else do you have to do?"

"Ah…" I say, shooting an involuntary glance out the front window, where there is, I'm sad to say, absolutely zero sign of Mia returning with the other women.

"Let's go, Liam," Ryker says, hooking an arm around my neck and pulling me into the library. "She's not going to get here any faster just because you have your nose pressed up against the window."

This generates a round of guffawing among the brothers, exactly the thing my plummeting morale needs right now.

"Fuck my life," I mutter, resigning myself to my fate.

More laughter at my expense.

Why not? None of us are feeling any pain at this point. I may as well enjoy some topnotch liquor on someone else's dime. Maybe I'll have a laugh. God knows I could use one. I'm sick of myself and my woe-is-me routine. It's like my head has turned into a broken TV with limited reception and the only thing I can watch is the Mia channel. Enough is enough. I'm tiptoeing dangerously close to loser territory.

The library, I should mention, looks like the sort of place where Bruce Wayne unwinds while waiting for someone to flash the Bat-Signal. Walls of shelves featuring leather-bound books. Ladders. Massive windows overlooking the beach. Tufted leather furniture.

We get settled. Ryker pours the drinks. Damon opens a big-ass cigar box.

"Who's having one?" He extracts the longest cigar I've ever seen in my life and extends it toward me. "Liam?"

"Nah." I wave a hand. "The last time I had one was at the bachelor party for a doctor from Ukraine I work with. Tried to keep up with him in the vodka department and wound up puking my guts out. Lost my taste for vodka *and* cigars."

"Tragic." Damon offers the cigar to Griffin. "Griff?"

Griffin puts his hands up and leans away as though he's being held at gunpoint. "Hard pass. Bellamy says I don't get laid tonight if I show up reeking of cigar smoke. That's a nonstarter."

A collective shudder goes around the group.

"Sacrifices must be made for the greater good," Ryker says, passing out the drinks. "Ella hates the smell of cigars, too, but I'm in the clear, since we're spending tonight apart. Looks like it's you and me, Damon."

"Are you kidding?" Damon says, grimacing. "If I have a cigar after that steak I just ate, I'll have indigestion until my next birthday. You're on your own."

With that, he hands the cigar to Ryker, snaps the box shut and has a seat.

Ryker sadly regards the cigar for a beat or two, then puts it back in the box and raises his glass.

"To pussies like us," he says heartily.

We all laugh and clink glasses.

"Hear, hear," Griffin says. He takes an appreciative sip, then zeros in on me with that laser-focused mischief. "So what's your issue? Can't be money. I saw your write-up in *Forbes*. You went public with your company and made a killing. Nice day's work."

"No issues here," I say, and the denial might have worked. But then Ryker opens his stupid mouth.

"He's hung up on an old girlfriend," he says. "She's here this weekend. The wedding dress designer."

"What the fuck?" I say, outraged by this flagrant disregard of the Men's Code and all it represents.

"Tomorrow you officially become my brother-in-law, which means you're family now," Ryker says. "I may as well throw you under the bus like I do with my other brothers. It's an honor. Trust me."

"Why don't I feel special?" I say, glaring at him.

"The wedding dress designer." Griffin furrows his brow. "Is that the Liv Tyler lookalike I saw earlier? You're punching above your weight, aren't you, champ? What have you got to offer a woman like *that*?"

More laughter at my expense. I know it's good-natured, but the joke hits a little too close to home. I think about my looks, which aren't bad, my career and my newly acquired fortune. And none of them have done me a damn bit of good when it comes to resolving my issues with Mia. Hell, I can barely get her to stay in the room with me and breathe the same air for ten minutes. And now she's seen my starlight tattoo and knows exactly how deep my loser-dom goes.

"You're not wrong," I tell Griffin.

"So what's the problem?" Damon asks. "Maybe we can help."

I quickly hold up a hand to stop this idea from gaining traction. "Pass. Things would have to be a hell of a lot worse and I'd have to be a lot drunker to get into personal details with *this* crew."

"What have you got to lose?" Griffin says. "We're drunk enough that we may or may not remember any of this tomorrow, so you're reasonably assured of our discretion. And we already know your deepest shame. Unless you have some nose-picking issue you haven't mentioned."

That's it for me. A guy can only take so much.

"Yeah, okay." I kill the rest of my drink and start to stand. "I'm out."

"Whatever you want." That's Ryker again, the glimmer of mischief in his eyes glowing brighter than ever. "You go on upstairs for more of your glum navel-gazing. I'm sure those two will think about you when they climb into bed with their women tonight. Matter of fact, maybe I'll ask the staff to send you some hot milk before you turn in. You'll need something to help keep warm tonight. Smart decision, Liam. I'd do the same thing."

Well, he's got me there. Their lives are great. Mine sucks.

And I need every ounce of help I can get. No matter how unlikely the source from whence it comes.

So I sit my ass back down, hand my empty glass to Ryker for a refill and decide to open up a little. No matter how much it pains me.

"I'm, ah, stuck." I rest my elbows on my knees and rub my hands together, staring at them so I don't have to see the brothers shoot me pitying and disgusted looks. Which I'm sure they're doing. "Can't live with her. Can't live without her. Can't get it figured out. Can't stop shooting myself in the foot."

"Ah," Damon says, nodding sagely. "Been there, done that. We all have."

This news is strangely cheering. I raise my head and frown at them, certain that I'm missing something.

"Don't bullshit me," I say. "The three of you never stop grinning like every day is Christmas at Disneyland. How'd you get so happy?"

"Easy," Griffin says dryly. "We just followed the stellar example set by our parents."

This sets off a round of laughter that sails right over my head.

"I don't get it," I say, my frown deepening. "What am I missing?"

"Our mom walked out on our dad for his best friend," Damon says with a wry grin.

"Whoa," I say, startled to discover that we all have much more in common than I'd thought. "My dad's mistress was Ella's mom. Let's just say *that* arrangement torpedoed my parents' marriage."

The brothers murmur sympathetically.

"So how did the three of you get your heads on straight with your relationships?" I ask.

"Kicking and screaming," Griffin says, grimacing.

"No, seriously," I say, my driving curiosity getting the best of me. I need help here, and I can't shake the sudden overwhelming feeling that there is valuable information for me to glean here. "What's your secret?"

"Our secret is, we saw the damage our parents did to each other and decided not to do that," Damon says. "A big part of learning the right thing to do is figuring out the wrong thing and avoiding it."

My brain scrambles hard, trying to keep up and produce some workable advice out of this, but it can't quite make that leap. I feel as though I'm standing on the rails of a treadmill running at ten miles per hour. I want to jump on, but I know I'm not ready.

"What does that *mean*?" I say.

"Listen," Griffin says, leaning toward me with a new level of urgency. No sign of that banked mischief now, which is a welcome relief. "Forget all that. There's one thing you need to focus on right now."

"Which is…?" I say impatiently.

"Pride," Griffin says. "Don't let it get in the way. Get rid of it. Pride is the enemy of a good relationship. Take it from me."

"Again," I say, not bothering to hide my frustration. "What does that *mean*?"

"It means that you need to go all in if you love this woman," Griffin says.

"Hang on." I lean against the cushions, backing away from the L-word. My stated plan for the weekend is to burn Mia out of my system for once and for all, and I plan to stick to that. Even if a whispery voice in my head keeps trying to tell me I'm lying to myself. "No one said anything about—"

"This right here?" Griffin nails me with exactly the sort of scathing look I feared. *"Pride.* I was proud, too. It took me a minute to admit that I need Bellamy. *Need* her. But I do. Why? Because she's smarter than me, and the two of us make a strong team. She pushes me to be better. It's not that she's trying to change me. It's that I *want* to be good enough for her. Why? Because she gets me. She's the best thing that ever happened to me. I'm not ashamed to admit it. I could pretend she's not and try to stumble through life on my own, but why? So my pride can win? Fuck that. And I'll tell you something else. My growth curve was painful. I'm not going to lie. But I'd do it over again a million times. To have what I have now with Bellamy? You bet your ass I would."

All that fervency from Griffin catches me by surprise.

Judging from the astonished looks on his brothers' faces, it catches *them* by surprise as well.

"*What?*" Griffin says when he realizes that the three of us are gaping at him.

"We can't believe how much you've changed. I think that's the most you've ever said about anything," Ryker says on behalf of the brothers. "Especially anything personal."

"Yeah, well," Griffin says, toasting us again before draining his glass. "Just goes to show how drunk I am."

That breaks us all up. We're still laughing when a new distraction arrives.

"Who's drunk?" comes a female voice and the drumming of heels on the floors. It's Ella, closely followed by Bellamy and Carly, Damon's fiancée. "Besides us, I mean."

A ripple of excitement goes through me and the others. There's nothing like the arrival of several beautiful women in sexy little dresses to supercharge a room full of men. True to form, Damon, Griffin and Ryker all light up like the Eiffel Tower on New Year's Eve. You'd think they hadn't seen their women for six months rather than two hours. Not that I'm any better. I hastily look around, threatening myself with a case of whiplash in my attempt to see what's going on in the hallway, but there's no sign of Mia. If I know anything about her, she's probably headed straight to her room in her determination to avoid any room with me in it.

The thought makes me sad.

Truly and deeply sad.

"Let's just say none of us would pass a breathalyzer test right now," Damon says, opening his arms to Carly, who slips into his lap for a hello kiss. "How was your dinner?"

"Delicious. How was yours?"

There's more, but I don't hear it. I get up and hurry out to the hallway, eager to find Mia and to turn my back on all the loving couples and their reunions. It's not that I'm not happy for them. I am. It's just that my personal life is already a nuclear waste site emitting a yellow glow and green smoke. I don't need any further reminders of what I don't have and can't figure out how to get.

There's no sign of Mia in the foyer or on the stairs, but I follow the sound of a door opening and discover her on the deck just off the formal living room. My heart rate accelerates like a 747 in the final seconds before wheels up as I stare at her through the French doors. She's beautiful, as always, but the dying light does something special to the blue highlights in her black hair as the breeze whips it past her face. Her profile as she watches the fiery sun setting against the rising tide seems tense. Pensive. As though she feels exactly as turbulent as I do.

Without stopping to think whether it's a good idea, I head outside and join her at the railing, Griffin's words of wisdom coming with me.

Pride is the enemy of a good relationship.

She hears my footsteps and doesn't seem at all surprised when she glances around and sees me.

A shiver of awareness passes through her. Subtle but there.

"Hey," I say, always the soul of eloquence where she's concerned.

"Hey."

"Spend the night with me." I trail my fingers down

the smooth column of her throat, savoring the way her flesh shivers beneath my touch. Silk and fire. And she thinks we can pretend this isn't here? "My room is the first one on the left. I'll be waiting for you."

"I told you," she says, keeping her attention fixed on the water. But I hear the subtle hitch in her breath and the huskiness in her voice. It may be inconvenient, but she wants me too. I know she does. "I keep telling you. It's not happening."

Not that again. Why do we have to keep playing these games?

"Fine. So you spend the night in your room thinking about me and I'll spend the night in my room thinking about you." Frustration creeps into my tone. "Brilliant."

"Yeah, well, I choose to be smart and horny over stupid and—"

She hastily cuts herself off, but sometimes I can hear the things she doesn't say. The important things she keeps hidden and locked up. This is one of those times.

"What? Brokenhearted?"

"We're done with this conversation."

"Look, I get it," I say. "You think that if you come tonight, I'll use it against you. You think I'll throw it in your face. And you're way too proud for that."

"Liam…"

"The thing you don't get is that what happens between you and me in the dark stays in the dark. It's just *us*. The same as it always was."

She hesitates before slowly turning her head to look at me. The evening's rosy glow provides enough illumination for me to see the uncertainty in her expression and, beneath that, the slow smolder of her desire.

"It's not just us. It's you, me and my regrets."

"Great," I say. "So you won't spend the night regretting turning down my offer?"

She stiffens and hastily looks away.

It would be so easy to walk away at this point, after her umpteenth rejection, but I can't. *Won't.*

"Do me a favor, Mia. Think about this when you're in bed alone but you can't sleep because you wish I had my mouth on your pussy."

"Liam."

I plow ahead, determined to get it all out there.

"I have pride issues, too. My pride isn't keen on me begging a woman to spend the night with me. But here I am. Trusting you not to throw it in my face. So maybe we're in this together. The same as we always were."

That's it. I've said all I can say right now.

She reluctantly faces me again. We stare at each other for a long moment, her ambivalence coming through as though she's given it a megaphone and told it to make a speech.

She opens her mouth. Hesitates.

"Liam…"

I experience the sudden violent urge to surrender to the flight response and turn tail and run.

I can't handle another rejection from her. I'm positive my soul would not survive it.

"I'll be in my room," I say, walking off before she can say anything else.

SHE'S NOT COMING, jackass.

I whack my pillow a couple of times and flop onto my back sometime after one, as the grim realization begins to pierce even my thick skull. Took me a while, but, hey, better late than never. She didn't come while I did roughly a thousand sit-ups and push-ups to burn off excess energy, took my shower, caught up on my work emails or mindlessly flipped channels. She didn't come at any point during the last hour or so, during which I tossed and turned my naked and aroused body from one side of the bed to the other. Hell, she's probably been fast asleep this whole time, peacefully snoozing away while I tie myself up in knots waiting for a miracle that's never going to happen. She probably had a good laugh at my expense before she fell asleep.

That Liam Wilder, boy. What a freaking idiot. I sure can play him, can't I?

My spirit sinks even further, circling the drain in my emotional toilet.

Are Guinness World Records still a thing?

Maybe I should nominate myself for the Biggest Fool category. I've got a real edge on the competition.

I toy with the idea of inviting myself down to her room, but even the new, pride-free version of me puts his foot down on that one. I went to her the last time. I can't do it all here without turning into an obsessed stalker. God knows I'm flanking the edge of that territory already.

I heave a harsh sigh, jacked up on disappointment, hormones and frustrated desire. My spine feels tense, as though it's been strung with one of those cables that they use for ski lifts.

I may as well try to get some sleep.

But first, I may as well jack myself off so I *can* sleep.

I lever myself up to sitting, reach under the covers and get to work beating my meat.

Which is how she finds me a few seconds later when she quietly slips inside my room, shutting and locking the door behind her.

She hesitates, surveying the scene. My hand slows as I survey *her*, every inch of my flesh prickling with awareness and adrenaline. There's enough moonlight filtering through the sheer drapes at the French doors for me to see her pale face. Her glittering eyes. The filmy robe that just skims her thighs as she moves closer. Those long legs. She brings a swish of silk with her as she comes. A whiff of that flower blend of hers drives me insane.

I don't know how any woman can stop a guy's heart and give him cardiac arrest at the same time, but *she* does. She always has.

"What are you doing?" she asks at the foot of the bed, her voice throaty.

"What do you think? I'm thinking about you. Wishing you were here."

She smiles, a white gleam of satisfaction in the night that's gone way too soon. "I'm here now."

"That you are." I get up on my knees, letting the covers drop, and stretch out a hand, reaching for her. "Come here."

Her movements are slow and easy as she undoes the belt and lets the robe slide off her body. She's tall and willowy. I've mentioned that. Her breasts are small, high and firm, dotted with perfect pink nipples that always perk for me when I look at them. Exactly like *that*. Her torso is long and lean, with exactly the right amount of curves. Her pussy? Bare. Her thighs? Toned and fit.

I open my mouth to tell her how beautiful she is and how often I think about her, exactly like *this*, but the only sound I can produce is a sharp intake of breath.

But that says it all, I suppose.

"You like what you see?" she says, running a hand through all that dark hair just to make sure she really drops me to my knees.

Guess I'm a better actor than I thought I was if she needs to ask.

"You could say that. Twelve years later, I still can't get enough of you."

"*Good.*"

The smugness in her voice compels me to reach over the side of the bed, grab her by the waist and toss her down beside me. I quickly straddle her, unleashing a little strength and enjoying her squeal of appreciative surprise.

"You like twisting me around your little finger?" I ask, using one of my hands to pin both of hers above her head. She writhes against me, straining to get free, but I'm not letting her go anywhere just yet. We have business to take care of together in this bed tonight, and we both know it.

Her hair forms a gleaming black halo, as though she's a dark angel.

Come to think of it, maybe that's *exactly* what she is.

She hikes up her chin, wild and defiant, even with me in the power position.

"I don't mind punishing you if I can."

"For...?" I ask, startled that she'd admit it.

"For breaking my heart."

"Easy mistake," I say without missing a beat, infuriated by her victim routine. As if she didn't give as good as she got and leave me for dead when she walked out of my life. "I didn't realize you had a heart to break. I never saw any sign of it."

She makes an outraged sound and bucks beneath me, letting me know I've hit the jackpot in riling her up. I call that winning. God knows I'll take any sort of passion she wants to throw my way. Anger works just fine. She gets a leg up between us. Maybe she's going for my groin. Who the hell knows? But I've got quick reflexes, and I don't take kindly to being attacked when I'm going to need my dick for important things in the next thirty seconds. I quickly let go of her hands and hook an arm behind her knee, spreading her wide and settling in the cradle between her thighs. A nice spot to grind against her tender pussy. Which is hot and wet, by the way. Her body reflexively arches and her breath catches as she reaches up to palm my cheeks.

I stare down at her, triumphant and euphoric as I let go of that knee, trail two fingers through her juices and, staring her in the face, suck my fingers deep into my mouth.

"Oh my God," she whispers, breathless, as she pumps against me as though her hips have a mind of their own. "You're going to make me come."

"That's the plan, Starlight."

"Do it," she says, spreading her legs wider. "Don't make me wait. And don't forget that this is just sex. Just scratching an itch. I'm still going to hate you when it's over."

Like I care.

Angry fucking may be twisted, sure. But if this is the only bone that she's tossing my way, I'm happy to take it and gnaw it to shards.

"Not so fast. You want to punish me? Knee me? Hate me? Have at it. You're never going to hurt me worse than you already have. Just stop acting like we're done with each other when we both know we're not. Are we?"

"Hurry, Liam," she says, pulling me closer.

"Not until you answer my question. We're not done with each other. *Are we?*"

She hesitates. Her mouth twists as though she can't quite force the words out.

"Maybe not. But it's not for lack of me trying."

"Try all you want." I can't stop a bitter laugh. God knows *I've* done my share of trying. "It'll never work."

"We'll see about that. Hurry, Liam."

There's no mistaking her urgency. Or mine.

I duck my head. She rises to meet me. We come together in a searing kiss, my tongue in her mouth and hers in mine. She groans helplessly. So do I. She scrapes her nails up my back and shoulders and across my scalp, pulling my hair. I work my way lower, sucking on her neck. On the sides of her breasts. Her nipples. A spot low on her belly, the one that's always driven her wild and made her taut muscles spasm and contract hard enough for me to feel.

There it is.

I laugh, triumphant.

Then I ease just a bit farther south, zeroing in on the deliciously slick spot that smells like fresh oysters.

I put my hungry mouth on her and work the hard little nub with my tongue. As always, this unleashes something wild inside her, causing her to latch on to my head and pull my hair in her frantic need to keep me right where I am, doing what I'm doing. So I keep doing it, until my entire body begins to tremble with the effort to keep myself in check and her incoherent cries above me announce that she's as close as I am.

By now I'm as frenzied as she is. I surge to all fours and lunge sideways for the foil packet on the nightstand. Then I set a new land speed record getting myself covered up. She watches me the whole time, propped up on her elbows, flushed and earthy, her lips and nipples swollen from my kisses. She's sweaty. She's sultry. She can't quite catch her breath. Neither can I. Nor can I believe my eyes or my good fortune.

Worse, I can't keep my stupid mouth shut. Some internal force wrestles me into submission and demands absolute truth. There's no shutting me up.

"I'm so lucky you're here with me again," I say as I settle on top of her and reach between us. "I can't believe I let you get away. We should've been together. The whole time. Exactly like *this*."

I thrust deep on *this*, burying myself to the hilt inside her silky heat. It's a snug fit with all her inner muscles

bearing down around me. The exquisite pleasure mush-
rooms until I can't swear that I don't pass out a little.
Meanwhile, she moans something indistinct that may
have my name inside it somewhere. I grind against her in
response, generating more helpless sounds from her. I
catch a glimpse of her wide eyes—she looks as shell-
shocked as I feel—then she slaps me hard on the ass and
my hips take over.

I fuck her hard, deep and fast. Just the way she likes
it. I urge her to wrap her legs around my waist, then urge
her to tighten them up. I fuse my lips with hers again,
absorbing her tongue and her cries into my mouth. I fuck
her until my thighs and lower back ache and the sound
of our flesh slapping together nearly drowns out everything else. Even my doubts and fears.

Until she crescendos with a single high note of astonishment that's an orgasm for my ears. I keep going
because I'm not satisfied with her level of satisfaction.
Sure enough, she stiffens and then shudders as her hips
spasm. Her cries ring through the room, loud and uninhibited. That's more like it. I hold myself in ruthless
check the whole time while she rides it out. Only when
she goes limp beneath me do I allow myself to catapult
over that edge with her. I sail through the darkness and
slam headfirst into ecstasy, producing a hoarse shout of
her name that seems to come from somewhere much
deeper than my throat.

Look. I'm a grown man with plenty of experience
under my belt. I know that great sex poisons the mind
and makes you see and feel things that aren't there. On
top of that, I know that I have a fatal weakness when it
comes to this one particular woman. Yet I know that this
whole "burning each other out of our systems with sex"

thing is absolute and unmitigated bullshit. I'm prepared to roll the dice on everything I own and swear that I am the one for her and she is the one for me. The *only* one. We may hate that. We may fight that. But we will never change that.

The idea terrifies me. So I do what I do, which is try my best to block it out.

When the lingering aftershocks finally wear off, I tumble to my side and collapse next to her, determined not to crush her when the strength in my trembling arms finally gives out. Then we lie side by side in the silence as our skin cools. Sadly, I'm too much of a coward to look her in the face and see if what just happened hit her the way it hit me.

Our breath eventually evens out. She doesn't say anything. *I* don't say anything. There's no telling what overblown declarations might leap out of my mouth if I try to speak right now, despite my desire to keep my feelings at a manageable level. I curse myself for letting her go without, say, hanging on to her hand. Because now I'm not touching her at all, and I can't figure out how to start that up again.

But I have to say *something*. Bad things happen when the two of us let too much silence open between us.

"The thing is…" I begin, trailing off when I catch myself about to stick my neck out again.

Jesus. Why can't I shut the hell up more often?

"What?" she asks quietly.

I roll to my side to face her and prop my head on my hand. I study her delicate profile. She studies the ceiling. I swallow hard and open my mouth, working against a tight throat and, worse, a complete lack of courage.

"The thing is, maybe we could talk now. Really talk. See what happens."

Her gaze finally meets mine, connecting me to a world of hurt and anger. It feels as though she's been stockpiling it all this time, collecting enough to fill a dumpsite and letting it marinate and rot. Seeing it now after the tenderness of the last few minutes is jolting, like following a rainbow to its end and discovering a malignant tumor rather than a pot of gold.

"You called me a *fucking lying bitch* when we broke up. Because you claimed I never loved you like I said I did. Remember that? You said you never wanted to see my *fucking face* again. I was kind of talked out after that."

I grimace at the reminder. I know I should apologize, but I can't quite manage it. My own wounds run too deep.

"I was twenty-two and immature. I was hurt," I say.

"I wasn't?"

Well, she's got me there. Funny how those two small words can support a ton of reproach.

We stare at each other, three inches apart on the bed and a universe of invisible barbed wire between us. I don't know what she's thinking, but I'm paralyzed and numb.

"Time for me to go," she says when I can't answer her question.

"Stick around," I say, forcing myself to reach for her hand and lace my fingers with hers. My reward for my bravery comes when she immediately squeezes my hand, almost as though she can't help herself. I'm so grateful for the tenderness that I'm ready to drop to my knees in gratitude. "You don't have to hurry off so soon."

Tired smile with maybe a hint of wistfulness from

Mia as she withdraws her hand. "I can barely forgive myself for letting you touch me again. I can't go down the rabbit hole of starting to care about you again. I'd never get over it."

So that's that. She's leaving. Again. No surprise there.

I withdraw my hands from her body and hold them up as though I've been burned. I suppose I have. I slump back against the pillows and watch as she hesitates there on the edge of the bed, looking around for her robe but not getting up just yet.

Griffin's stupid words about pride rattle around in my head again. If I had a little more pride, I wouldn't be sitting here with the renewed sensation that my guts have just been ripped out and that I've said way too much.

On the other hand...

On the other hand, my blood still runs hot and my skin still feels alive the way it only ever feels when she's in the room. I'm still drunk enough that my defenses aren't as high as they should be. And the two of us will never get past all the roadblocks in our way if one of us doesn't have a little more courage.

Might as well be me.

"You're killing me," I say, roughly running my hands over the top of my head because it keeps them from reaching for her again. "Do you get that? Do you care?"

She glances back at me over her shoulder, her skin pale in the moonlight. Maybe the liquor is making me imagine things that aren't there, but I swear I see the shimmer of tears in her eyes and a slight tremble in her chin as she opens her mouth and waits for her words to catch up.

"If I thought you meant it? I *would* care." She laughs shakily and looks at the ceiling. Maybe she's hoping God is lurking up there somewhere, ready to swoop in with some answers or some suggestions on how to break this permanent impasse between us. "I'm so stupid when it comes to you that it would mean everything to me."

Stupid. Huh. Yeah.

There's a lot of that going around. Probably why I feel this euphoric surge of hope. Because something is still there. And I can work with her if there's *something*. We can forgive each other and put this thing back together if there's *something*.

"*Mia,*" I say, easing closer—

She stiffens and surges to her feet. Away from me. Her expression is hard now. Unforgiving.

"But I don't believe anything you say to me anymore, Liam. Part of me wants to, but I don't."

"We can work on that," I say, continuing my stupid streak.

"That's the problem," she says, as heartless and cruel as she ever was, despite what just happened in this bed. Maybe there's a tinge of regret there for slamming the emotional door in my face, but it's nowhere near enough. "I don't want to work on it."

9

NATURALLY, I toss and turn for most of the night. I have no way of proving it, but I believe I fall asleep approximately thirty seconds before my alarm goes off. I stare at the weak early morning sunlight trying to make its way past the drapes and curse the dark fate that has brought me to this wretched point in my existence.

On top of the whole Liam debacle, I have to spend another *day* immersed to the eyeballs in happy couples, all of whom are in various stages of living out their romantic dreams. Speaking on behalf of all miserable single people everywhere in the world, the worst day of our lives was when some idiot first came up with the idea of a wedding weekend as opposed to a wedding day. I can only manage so much happiness for other people when my own personal life is a turd factory. Isn't it enough that I survived dinner with the girls last night and will somehow survive the wedding and reception later? Why do I also need to be subjected to a pre-wedding breakfast, massages and mani-pedis, hair and makeup *and* a post-wedding breakfast tomorrow? I barely know these people! I'm only here because I designed the bride's dress and struck up a fledgling friendship with her. How much small talk and chitchat can I possibly generate? And all while pretending not to notice all the googly-heart eyes that Damon and Carly, Griffin and Bellamy and Ryker and Ella keep throwing each other's way? Every one of these couples needs to find a room and stay there. If I stumble on one more stolen kiss or ass grab, I'm going to start smashing some fine china around here.

I'm telling you, people ask too much of their wedding guests. Way too much.

I stare blearily at the ceiling, trying without much success to generate enough energy to get up.

My thoughts naturally drift to Liam…to last night… to my efforts to block him out a little and keep some of my thoughts, heart and body to myself. To establish a relationship that's a little more arm's-length and a lot less all-consuming. An effort that has never worked, going all the way back to that first time I met him on the plane.

After the comment about how special I am, we lapse into an awkward silence. I get the feeling that he wishes he hadn't said so much about his personal life. I also get the feeling that he's a massive flirt. I'm sure there was a time, not that long ago, when Janet felt dazzled and starstruck looking into the same extraordinary hazel eyes. This is not the sort of guy who's big on commitment. A smart girl would remember that. And let's just say that I didn't get into NYU's design program on the basis of my looks. So I ignore him during takeoff. When we reach our cruising altitude, I pull out my markers and start sketching designs on my pad, pretending I don't feel the steady touch of his attention on the side of my face. At some point, he produces the New England Journal of Medicine *and flips through it.*

"So we're working now?" he finally says, a tinge of exaspera-tion in his voice. "No more talking?"

Excitement flares through me. So much for being smart.

Maybe if I don't look directly at him while we talk…?

"Speak freely," I say, still sketching. "I can do two things at one time."

"You're really good," he says, leaning across the armrest and causing our arms to touch. "I don't know anything about fash-ion. Or wedding dresses. But that looks amazing."

"Thanks," I say, flushing with pleasure.

"So is this your thing? Wedding dresses?"

"Getting hired out of college so I can pay off my exorbitant student loans is my thing," I say wryly.

"Hmm."

I take a sharper look at his face, which now appears vaguely guilty. He'd be terrible trying his hand at professional poker in Vegas.

"Hang on," I say, narrowing my eyes at him. "You're a trust fund baby, aren't you?"

"No comment," he says, making a real project out of avoiding eye contact and flipping through my sketches. "We're talking about you. And wedding dresses."

"I do love them," I say, deciding to let him off the hook. For now.

"They're your favorite?"

"They are."

"Why?"

"Because they're challenging," I say, making the mistake of looking directly up at him. Our arms are still touching. Our faces are close together. I note a couple of golden freckles across his nose, so faint that you'd miss them if you were at any sort of a distance. Then I note the tender curve of his lip. People talk about these moments where chemistry sizzles between people, but that's not the moment when my heart stops.

"Hold up," he says, frowning. "Wedding dresses are your favorite. And you're good at them. You gotta find a way to make it work. Open your own studio or something. Otherwise, I feel like you'll be depriving the world of something. And you'll never be satisfied with your career."

Like it's just that easy.

Actually, maybe it is if you're rich like he is rather than a solidly middle-class person whose parents mortgaged their house to the roof for the opportunity to send me and my brother to NYU.

"I appreciate your support and encouragement, but that costs money. Which I do not have. And you're just flirting because you hope to get laid when we land. You've got an empty space to fill now that you've fired Janet, but you don't have your eye on an Italian girl yet, so you're a little worried. And, by the way, you should know that I know all about you and your romantic exploits. My brother is Michael Jamison. He tells me almost everything."

"Oh, so you're Mia."

"I am. Mia Nova Jamison. At your service."

"How did you know who I am?"

"Saw your name on your ticket just now."

"Sneaky. Wonder why our paths haven't crossed on campus by now?"

"Because you're in engineering and I'm in design," I say. "And because you party and I don't."

"True. Your brother talks about you all the time. Good stuff."

"Yeah?" I say, my cheeks tingling with pleasure. "What about you? Siblings?"

"Half-sister," he says with some reluctance. "We're not close. Not like you and Michael."

"You could change that," I say, because this seems to matter to him a great deal. "And you can build your own family. So you're not stuck with the one you're stuck with."

"I'll have to think about that."

He's still staring. There seems to be a fair amount of quiet disbelief in his expression now. I get the feeling he doesn't know what to make of me any more than I know what to make of him.

"Anyway, Michael has told some stories about your adventures that would make your hair uncurl," I say, eager to get back onto steadier ground.

He makes a face. "Bear in mind that everything I tell your brother and my other friends has a built-in exaggeration factor of about fifty percent. Just to make myself look good to the other idiots."

I grin. "Noted. That still makes you a bad boy. And a player. I'm sure Janet would agree."

He shrugs, unrepentant. "A guy's gotta pass the time until the right woman shows up."

"Indeed," I say gravely. "A guy doesn't want to be lonely for two seconds."

There's a long pause while he studies me, a bemused and vaguely stunned look settling in for a long stay on his face. He studies me for so long that my cheeks begin to burn.

"I have a question," he finally says, his voice quiet. "Am I going to have to fight your brother if I want to spend some time with you? I don't want any issues."

"Unknown," I say, battling a sinking sensation that feels suspiciously like disappointment. Even if he was the right kind of guy for me, which he's decidedly not, he wouldn't want to step out of line by hooking up with a friend's sister. That's an ironclad part of the unwritten code between men. Everyone knows that. "Nothing's ever happened between me and one of his friends before."

"I also don't want to get my face caved in. So let me know if you think it'll be an issue. I can start boxing at the gym."

My foolish heart swoops. "That's a lot of trouble for you to go through until your right girl shows up," I say, trying hard to control my smile.

"Maybe she's here," he says, not smiling.

He's only flirting, *I sternly warn myself.* He doesn't mean it.

Anyway, a guy like this and a girl like me? Unlikely.

"I can hear your thoughts, Mia Nova," he says, tapping my temple and generating a shower of electrical sparks across my scalp. "Any chance I might like you?"

"Minimal," I say with a shaky attempt at a laugh, undone both by his intuitiveness and my transparency.

But he's not laughing.

A faint frown shadows his face as he stares at me. I don't know what he's looking for, but he sure is trying hard to find it. And I find it impossible to look away.

"Please tell me your boyfriend is way at the back of the plane," he says quietly. "Or, better yet, back home."

"I don't have a boyfriend," I say, breathless.

"Good," he says, already reaching for my face. "I'm going to call you Starlight. Hope you don't mind."

"I don't mind," I whisper.

He palms my cheeks, lowers his head and gives me a second to adjust to the idea that he's coming in, as though I'd scream or ring for the flight attendant. Then he kisses me. His lips are lush. Persistent. Persuasive. The hands on my face telegraph his growing tension and latent power. I'm sure my helpless hum of pleasure tells him everything he needs to know. He doesn't use his tongue. He doesn't need to.

By the time we pull apart, I feel overheated. Dazed.

He looks bewildered.

He lets me go by pulling his hands back as though he's been zapped. Then he seems not to know what to do with his hands and runs them through his hair, ruffling it as he slumps back against his seat.

"Shit," he says, eyeing me with unfiltered desire, bewilderment and what looks like a wary new respect. "This is going to be more complicated than I thought."

That's *the moment my heart stops.*

Because I know he's exactly right.

I blink my attention away from the ceiling, coming out of it.

All this time later, and things are still complicated.

I rub my face hard, doing my best to wipe away the memory's lingering sweetness and the resulting ache. In my heart rather than any parts further south.

I roll out of bed and pull myself together enough to throw on my workout gear and running shoes. Then I hit the beach, drained and cranky. Luckily, there are compensations. It's a glorious morning out here in the Hamptons, with the sunlight glittering like broken crystal across the water. The breeze kicks in. Seagulls swoop and dive. My mood lifts with the rhythmic pounding of my feet on the sand. I do three miles up and back without too much effort. The house returns to view. I'm in the home stretch, spurred to pick up my pace by the sight of caterers setting up a breakfast buffet on the deck. I'm just beginning to think that things aren't *quite* as bad as I'd thought and that I have the energy to make it through another day or so of wedding delirium when I hear it.

The fast-approaching sound of another runner.

My heart sinks because I know. I just *know*. I don't even bother looking around to confirm my suspicions and make sure I'm not about to be accosted by some local criminal. Honestly, that would be a relief at this point. Anything to save me from another fraught interaction with *him*, especially with this shameful and insidious surge of excitement running through me to see him again.

But no. I'd never get that lucky.

"Morning, Mia Nova," Liam says in his husky just-woke-up voice.

He slows his pace as he falls into stride beside me. I see, out of the corner of my eye, that he's wearing gray shorts, a sweaty white T-shirt, Aviator shades and a basketball hat like me. Only he sports a Miami Heat cap while mine is the Brooklyn Nets. The field of heat radiating from his big body is unsettling, but not as unsettling as his scent, which is a dizzying version of his usual linen and soap combo. I guess the warmth of his skin carries superpowers that turn every little smell into a pheromone to attract the weak and unsuspecting. Like me. Right on cue, I feel the curl of desire as it begins its slow spiral in my belly and parts lower.

Sucks to be me right now. Swear to God. I can't even.

"Sleep well?" he continues.

"I slept great," I say brightly.

"Yeah, me neither," he says. "I always sleep better with you."

Sure he does. It's all I can do not to shove him face-first into the sand.

"You look remarkably energetic for someone who hasn't slept for twelve years," I say.

"I do what I can to struggle through."

"No doubt," I mutter. "Don't let me keep you. I know my pace is much lower than yours."

"No worries. I think I can manage. We used to run together all the time, remember? I'm cooling down anyway."

"Wonderful."

"Remember that day we jogged around the Colosseum? Then got gelato on the way home? You got pistachio. You always got pistachio."

And he always got stracciatella. That was his favorite.

I keep my eyes straight ahead and pretend I don't feel the unbearable pang of nostalgia in my belly.

"Oh, was that you?"

"Do you ever think about all the things we have in common? *Still* have in common? We're athletic. We like to swim. We like to run. Both live for basketball. I see you still haven't found a decent team, though. Sadly."

"First of all, screw the Heat. Second, harass *me* all you want. Leave the Nets out of it."

He grins, leaving me a bit more devastated and undone. "It was a tough choice, by the way. Following you the rest of the way and staying back there where I can enjoy the view—can't decide whether I like your legs or your ass the best, just so you know—or catching up to you."

I scowl. "Why not stay back there? Then you could keep doing whatever it is you're doing without disturbing my peace."

This time, *he* scowls. "Because, like it or not—and I *don't* like it—I have more fun with you than with anyone else I've ever met. I couldn't resist."

I slow to a walk as I near the bottom of the stairs leading to the deck, shooting him a sidelong glare. I find

it exhausting to keep reminding myself that he doesn't
mean it when he says things like this, no matter how
sincere he seems. He's honed his soulful honesty routine
to an art form. That doesn't mean I have to buy it.

"A rookie mistake," I say. "No one's more fun than I
am. If we're done here…?"

"We're not, actually."

He stops and sidesteps to block me from going any
further. To my dismay, he takes off his sunglasses and
hooks them into his collar, then takes the bottom half of
his T-shirt and uses it to wipe his sweaty face. I'm
tempted to glance at those rippling abs, but those breath-
taking eyes are laser focused on me now and keep me
riveted. All signs of mischief are gone, alerting me to the
fact that the lighthearted banter section of the proceedings is over.

Liam's dead serious now.

I catch myself holding my breath while I wait to see
what he does next.

I don't dare take my eyes off him. Not for a *second*.

"This will probably surprise you, Starlight, because I
know you think I'm a monster, but I have feelings.
Almost like a regular human being does."

"*You* have feelings?" I ask, desperate to keep him at
arm's length and to remain unmoved by the wounded
note in his voice. I can deal with his anger without any
problem. His seeming vulnerability? I can no more
manage that than I could manage a breath mint laced
with plutonium. "If you say so."

"I do. It's taken some guts for me to reach out to you
again. And to touch you. And every time I've talked to
you and confessed what I'm feeling."

I feel an unwelcome and ridiculous pang of guilt as I

think about how I've rebuffed him. Repeatedly and with unrestrained bitchery.

"Liam…"

"So I was kinda hoping you'd go easier on me when I said I wish I hadn't let you go. But you didn't. And you know what? That's fine."

I watch him warily, battling a creeping feeling of dread that wants me to back up a step or two and put some distance between me and his determination to get to whatever point he's making. I'm not going to like whatever he says next. I'm not going to like it *a lot*.

He eases closer, getting in my face. Everything else in my world drops away except for the hard glint of turbulence in his eyes.

"As long as you understand that *I* don't believe you when you tell me bullshit like you don't want to work on things. That's what kept me staring at the ceiling for most of the night. *Did Mia really mean that? Is she really fine with a fuck-buddy relationship? Is she really over what we had together?* But then it hit me. You're protesting way too much."

See? What did I tell you? I don't like this at *all*.

"Wow. So you're a mind reader now," I say quickly.

"Nope. Just a student of history. And that's a thing you do whenever I get too close. You protest. You did it on the plane when we first met. You've done it nonstop since I came back to town. You did it last night. Hell, I don't know. Maybe you're trying to convince yourself. But I'm not fooled. I won't be fooled. Once I realized that last night? I slept like a baby."

"Well, o-kay, then," I say, my cheeks burning with humiliation rather than from the sun's heat. I can never have a private thought when it comes to Liam. He's never allowed me to keep a feeling to myself and hide it away somewhere for later examination. He sees *everything*. "Thank you for that *thoughtful* analysis. I'm dying for some coffee. So if there's nothing else…?"

His jaw tightens. "I'm. Not. Fooled. And here's another thing. I'm sick of your presence in my life. You're like a shadow over everything."

"*What?*"

"I'm thirty-four years old now. Do you know how many women I've dated?"

The idea fills me with seething hostility.

"I can only imagine. Your point?"

"My point is that every one of them gets compared to you. You're like the platinum standard in my life that I never asked for. *Is she as smart as Mia? As funny as Mia? As sexy as Mia? Does she understand me the way Mia used to understand me? Does she make me feel the way I used to feel with Mia? Can I ever get that feeling back?*"

I gape at him, stunned by his fervency and fresh out of snarky comebacks.

He doesn't mean any of that that, does he?

"I mean it, Mia! I. Mean. It. I'm sick of trying to find what *you* have in some other person," he says, his voice rough with righteous fury. "I'm sick of being stuck in the same phase of my life. How many more women do you expect me to go through? How much energy do you think I have? I'm sick of knowing we had something so great but now it doesn't count because we ruined it. I can't deal with this asterisk in my life anymore. It's like I found the world's biggest diamond. I had it in my *hands*. I saw all the possibilities. But then I dropped it and lost it." Self-deprecating laugh without a touch of humor in it. "And now I'll never know what might have been if I wasn't so unbelievably immature and *stupid*."

I can't move. Can't think, can't talk, can't *breathe*. It takes all my energy to stand there and blink back the hot tears that keep trying to fall.

I want to scream, run away and hide.

I want to fall into his arms and swear that I'll do anything—*anything*—to hold up my half of our sky so we can work our way back to where we used to be.

I open my mouth. Nothing comes out.

"And you melt when I touch you and look at me the way you always used to look at me when you think I'm not looking, but then tell me you don't want to work on it? You expect me to believe that *you* don't have an asterisk in *your* life just like *I've* got one in *mine*?"

An asterisk.

Have I got an *asterisk* in my life?

Is that why I kinda like the men I date and kinda enjoy the sex and kinda open to them but keep a corner of myself boxed off and untouchable? Is that why I've moved to a succession of bigger and better apartments with nicer and more expensive stuff yet never feel that I'm home at the place where I belong and need to stay? Is that why no amount of career success or friends or money has ever made a dent in the yawning loneliness that follows me wherever I go?

An *asterisk*?

Could Liam be the missing puzzle piece to all of that?

What a terrifying idea.

More terrifying? Gooseflesh rises all over my body because I know the truth is in the air somewhere nearby.

"What do you want me to say?" I ask quietly. "You want me to tell you that I'm okay with everything that happened? You want me to be happy that I still think about you even though I know I shouldn't?"

Something in his expression softens, generating those sexy crow's-feet at the corners of his eyes and a responsive warmth inside me that's entirely separate from the sun's rays now beating down on us.

"Nope. I'm not expecting a beach miracle on my sister's wedding day, Mia Nova. But when the wedding's over tonight, we need to talk. Really talk. See if we can put some stuff behind us once and for all."

The suggestion that we open up all those old wounds leaves me cold and terrified. It's one thing to try to start something new and build it from here, something else again to go back to all the ugliness and rehash it when it did more than enough damage the first time.

But…

Maybe it's a pipe dream or a delusion to think we can build a solid new house on a cracked foundation.

Still, that's the thing with Liam. He always wants *more* from me. He always goes too far.

So much for progress.

"I'm not doing that," I say flatly, sidestepping him and heading up the stairs.

"Meet me in my room after the reception," he calls behind me, and there's not a hint of compromise in it. "Don't make me come looking for you."

10

I DIDN'T GET to be a successful cardiac surgeon by falling apart in tense situations. Trust me on that. If some dude on a crowded flight turns up with shooting pains in his left arm and across his chest and his companion shouts out a frantic *We need a doctor over here!*, I'm the guy you hope answers the call. Same thing with gruesome car accidents, where someone threatens to bleed out by the side of the road before the EMTs arrive. I'd probably also be great at a hostage negotiation or talking a would-be jumper down from a ledge. I'm fine with snakes, spiders, heights and public speaking.

In short, I'm generally a cool cucumber. Shit doesn't get to me.

Normally.

So you and Martha Stewart will probably both laugh your asses off to discover that weddings are my own personal kryptonite.

I'm dead serious.

Every time one of my buddies gets married (and most of them are married by now, the fuckers), I take another journey through the seven rings of hell. Starting with signing the stupid guestbook at the ceremony and ending with the spectacle of watching grown adults tackle each other for the pleasure of capturing a used bouquet of flowers while their partner, more often than not, tries to hide in the shadowy perimeters of the ballroom and/or freezes with a wooden smile of horror affixed to their face.

Weddings make me tense into a tuxedo-wearing block of cement. No lie.

I do not want to see ribbons, flowers or candles. I do not want to eat cake. I do not want to raise a glass of champagne in a toast.

And the biggies?

I do not want to sit quietly by and watch another couple stare lovingly into each other's eyes and promise forever while also remembering the silent hostility between my father and my mother. Who, surprisingly, did not approve of his mistress and love child.

I do not want to remember the way Mia—

"Liam. You ready? It's showtime."

Startled out of my morose thoughts, I do my best to block them out and glance around to discover the happy groom watching me. Everyone else has gone downstairs already, evidently. Matter of fact, I now hear the strains of a string quartet playing Pachelbel's Canon in the huge foyer, where the ceremony will take place momentarily beneath a monster arch of flowers that they set up earlier. Ryker's standing at the bedroom door and looking back at me as though I'm crazy. Which I probably am.

"Right behind you," I say, blinking myself out of my shitty mood and trying to manage a smile as we walk down the long hallway toward the stairs. Actually, *he* floats and *I* trudge, which isn't the look I'm going for on the happiest day of my sister's life. I decide I need to make a bigger effort, so I put more perk in my voice. "Got the rings?"

"Right here," he says, patting his pocket.

"Good man," I say, clapping him on the back.

"Listen." He stops and turns to face me, catching me by surprise with his sudden fervor. "I just want to tell you. You never have to worry about Ella with me. I'll take great care of her. I'm the luckiest guy in the world. I want to make sure she feels like the luckiest woman. Every single day."

I hesitate, caught off guard by this proclamation.

This is the kind of syrupy shit I could do without in my current state of mind. It's fine for all the brothers Black and their significant others to wallow in their excruciating happiness today as long as they give me a wide berth and leave me the hell out of it. And it's not that I'm not happy for them. I am. It's just that I'm barely hanging on by a thread as I try to keep my head above the miserable waters of trying to figure out whether Mia and I will ever work things out. And every happy couple here is a reminder of what I don't have and may never have.

A best friend. A partner. A lover. A *home*.

A future worth getting excited about.

Imagine my surprise, then, to discover myself feeling unexpectedly touched by Ryker's evident sincerity.

He means it. He plans to mean it for the rest of his life.

Isn't that the best anyone can ask for? Isn't this exactly what a great woman like Ella deserves?

But...

It's strange being the recipient of a vow like this. I know I'm the only male relative she has left, but I'm not her father. Our father is gone and she she's only recently begun acknowledging me as her brother. True, she asked me to escort her down the aisle today, so that's a hopeful sign. Still, I feel like I'm taking something that doesn't belong to me.

Time for me to set the record straight.

"You don't have to—"

"Yeah." Ryker never breaks eye contact. "I do."

Here's another thing I hate about weddings: they make my emotions rise way too close to the surface, where it's so much harder to keep them in check.

I clear my throat, which has suddenly turned tight. "Good to hear."

I turn to continue down the hall, determined to make my escape from this conversation before my eyes start burning. But there's more.

"And I meant what I said last night," Ryker says. "Ella's brother is *my* brother. Even a half-brother."

To my utter astonishment, he pulls me in for a bear hug, gives me a firm kiss on the cheek, then concludes with, yes, more bear hugging.

Well, *shit*.

I'm messed up by the time he turns me loose. There's an embarrassing quiver in my chin. An unwelcome haze over my vision. I would've been fine with either the speech *or* the hug and kiss. I could have inserted an asterisk into this whole conversation and convinced myself that he was only about fifty percent sincere, which is the appropriate amount to use on a half-brother like me who only recently showed up in his sister's life.

But with both the speech *and* the hug and kiss? Either he really means it or he's a great actor.

Either way, I don't know what to say or do.

I'm shocked to discover, in my mid-thirties, when I should be well past this kind of sentimentality, how much it means to me to be welcomed into a family that seems nice. And...normal-ish. Not at all like the one I grew up in, where the toxicity between my mother and father practically required a hazmat suit and an EPA cleanup.

"Whatever you say." I clear my throat and hope it works on some of the gruffness in my voice. "Having met your brothers, I can't see why you want any more of them, but... I'll take it."

We both laugh, which lightens the mood. Thank God.

"You'd better get going," I say. "You wouldn't want to miss the part where you stand in front of everyone looking awkward while you wait for her to walk down the aisle."

"Yeah, I know," he says, eyeballing the closed door of Ella's rooms, where the women are getting dressed and from whence they'll shortly emerge. "Hang on a sec. I just need to..."

To my horror, he knocks on the door.

I'm no expert on wedding rituals, but even *I* recognize the signs of a disaster in the making when I see them.

"What the hell are you doing?" I bark. "You know brides freak out if you try to see them before the ceremony."

"It'll be okay," he says in what I consider to be a naïve display of optimism.

"Why am I hearing male voices outside my room?"

calls my sister from the other side of the door. "Ryker? Is that you?"

"It's me," he says sheepishly.

"You're not about to duck out the back door, are you?" Ella says, sounding worried. "Because Mia's already strapped me into this dress and I've given myself a pep talk on getting down the stairs in these heels without killing myself. If you're going to cancel, you should've done it half an hour ago."

"I'm not canceling on you, sunshine. You know that," Ryker says, grinning.

"Make sure you don't," Mia says, laughing. "I don't need the humiliation — *Hey. What're you doing?*"

Ryker and I exchange bemused looks as we hear the sounds of a minor scuffle inside the room. Then the door flies open without warning. Out steps Ella's Aunt Gilda, whom I met yesterday afternoon. She's striking in a silvery dress that sets off her spiky white hair. Unfortunately for Ryker, she also bears more than a passing resemblance to a snarling rat terrier as she quickly snaps the door shut again.

"What are you doing?" she demands of Ryker, hiking her chin as though she plans to take a swing at him. "You're not about to say anything to Ella that'll make her cry, are you? Because the makeup artist is already downstairs, and we can't have any dripping or smudging before the ceremony."

"Relax, Aunt Gilda," he says. "I'd never upset Ella before the wedding."

"Aunt Gilda, I am a *grown* —" an outraged Ella calls from inside the room.

"That also includes saying anything to her that would

make her cry tears *of joy* before the ceremony," Aunt Gilda tells Ryker, pointing at his nose.

"I'll do my best, but no promises," Ryker says with a tinge of exasperation. "Can I talk to my bride for a sec? Before you make us both late for our own wedding?"

This magic combination of words gets Aunt Gilda to stand down. "Be my guest," she says with a benevolent nod before smoothing both of Ryker's lapels and giving his black tie a minute adjustment. "You're quite the handsome devil when you clean up, by the way. Give us a kiss."

"You look gorgeous," Ryker says, looking relieved. He gives her a quick kiss and hug. "Get out of here. See you downstairs."

"See you downstairs." She starts to bustle off, then pauses. "Ella, don't you forget to smile on your way down. Otherwise your pictures will be ruined."

"Oh my *God*," Ella says.

"I'm off," Aunt Gilda says with an airy wave as she disappears down the steps.

"Ryker?" Ella calls. "You still there?"

"Yep. One sec," Ryker says, shooting me a quick frown. "Could you, uh…"

"Where the hell am I supposed to go?" I say with vague alarm. I don't want to be part of this touching love scene any more than they want me here, but my options are severely limited. "I'm supposed to walk her down in three seconds."

"Just wait down there," he says, pointing back up the hallway the way we just came.

Like *that's* going to do any good when he needs to keep his voice up so she can hear him through the door.

I retreat as far as I can, turning my back on them and bracing for the worst.

The lovebirds, meanwhile, begin their mutual cooing.

"Missed you last night," Ryker tells her, his voice sweetening by the syllable.

"Missed *you*," she says. "We'll make up for it tonight."

I cringe.

"Indeed we will. Just to make sure everything is legal. Word is you made us a nice chocolate ganache cake for the reception. We'll have to put that to good use later, so make sure to save a big piece."

"I can't wait," she says with a dreamy sigh.

For fuck's sake.

I retreat another step or two up the hallway and stare out the nearest window, idly considering the possibility of jumping before I hear anything else about my sister's sex life that I won't be able to un-hear. At this point, a grievous injury would be a small price to pay.

"Anyway, I just wanted to say…" Ryker trails off, his voice cracking at the end. Whoa. I can hear the tears in his voice loud and clear. "I just wanted to say… Thank you. For blessing my life. You're *everything*. You know that?"

"You promised not to make me cry," she says with a shaky laugh and a sniffle. "And why would you thank *me*? Did you think there was someone else I wanted to be with?"

"I don't know," he says, then clears his throat. "Hard to believe I got this lucky."

"Good thing you didn't take no for an answer that night at Bemelmans when we first met, huh?" she says.

More laughter while I resist the overwhelming urge to stick my fingers in my ears.

"I'd better get down there," he says, much to my relief. "See you in a minute. Love you."

"Love you," Ella calls.

I'm standing there wondering if the coast is clear enough for me to risk turning around when Ryker speaks at a normal volume.

"I'm counting on you to make sure she gets safely down the steps, Liam," he says. "If she trips and breaks an ankle, it's *your* ass. We've got a honeymoon to enjoy."

"Aye, cap," I say, facing him with a crisp salute.

He lobs a final pointed glance in my direction, then takes off down the steps. Finally. Freeing me up to knock on my sister's door to see if she's ready.

"Come in," she says, swinging the door open.

"As brother of the bride, I shouldn't be subjected to —" I freeze as I get a good look at her. "*Holy shit*. You look amazing."

"You sure?" she asks anxiously, fluffing up her veil. "What about the heels? They're Manolos."

I have no idea what that means, but I play along as she lifts her hem, showing off fancy blue heels with bows.

"I'm positive," I say. "He's going to lose it when he sees you. Guaranteed."

"From your lips to God's ears," she says with a glorious bride's grin.

"Not sure those heels are street legal for a bride, though," I add. "Aren't they supposed to be white?"

"I like a little flair," she says as we laugh together.

I'm seriously trying to hold it together here, but it's not getting any easier as this endless day wears on. I don't believe in angels, but my sister in her wedding dress comes close. And I don't know anything about wedding dresses, but I sure as hell know spectacular when I see it. Ella on her wedding day is *spectacular*. She's got the veil over her face. A little tiara with her hair up. The gown is pretty plain, with no fussy lace or beads, but it's a blinding white material—satin, maybe—that really catches the eye. She looks like Cinderella. Or a fairy princess. And I hope to God that Mia charges wealthy brides at least five figures for a dress like *this*, because I know they'd be happy to pay it.

A shitload of emotions collects into a lump in my throat.

"I just want to say one thing," she says, taking both my hands in hers and giving them a squeeze.

"What's that?" I say gruffly.

"I'm so glad you're in my life now." I glimpse the shimmer of tears behind her veil and detect a slight wobble in her smile. It's all I can do to stop myself from losing it as I unexpectedly think about our father. I don't know if he's looking down on us or anything like that, but I'm sure he would've done anything to be here in my place and walk Ella down the aisle. "I didn't know how much I needed my brother. But I do. And I just wanted to mention that before we go downstairs and things get crazy. I'm glad you're here, Liam."

Well, *shit*.

"Me too." I pause, wishing I knew who put all that gravel in my voice. "You deserve all the happiness, Ella. I'm glad you found a good guy who worships the ground you walk on."

"I just want you to be as happy as I am."

I want to say *fat chance*, but I'm trying not to be a cynical asshole on her big day. I open my mouth, gearing up to respond with a simple *thank you* instead, when the bathroom door swings open and out walks Mia.

I freeze, my head emptying out until only cotton fluff, lost dreams and bitterness remain.

Swear to God, Mia brings as much sweet misery to my life as she does longing and naked lust.

Why? Let me count the ways.

First, I hoped she was downstairs already and that I therefore had a few more minutes to get my mind right.

Second, I know that no one outshines a bride, but when Mia is in the room, there's nowhere else for me to look. Today's black dress is a plain number that I'm sure she designed herself and looks as though it came from Jackie Kennedy's closet. Miles of long legs. Gleaming skin. Flowing black hair that's a bit curlier than usual. Fire-engine-red lips.

Third, and this is a biggie, there's something about seeing her in the room on a wedding day with a wedding dress—even if she's not wearing it—that makes my equilibrium spin like a top.

I'm not trying to be dramatic here. I'm a grown man. I normally have no problems acting like one. But standing there, still trapped inside my endless purgatory, I'm not sure how much longer I can function without making peace with Mia.

I just don't think I have it in me.

"I'll go wait on the landing," Ella says, successfully reading the room and slipping away, her dress rustling.

I barely notice.

I take a deep breath and swallow my pride, even though Mia terrifies me and I'm also not sure how much more rejection I can take.

"Hey," I say.

"Hey," she says, a pretty blush creeping over her cheeks.

"Great job on Ella's dress."

"Thank you," she says, ducking her head and smoothing her hair. She seems to have a tough time looking me in the eye. The feeling is mutual, trust me. "She seems happy with it."

"You look amazing."

"So do you," she says with a hint of a smile. "I'd better go. I need to make sure her train is straight."

That almost-smile catches me off guard. It gives me hope. Which is why I lose my head a little when she starts to follow Ella.

I put a hand on Mia's arm before I think better of it, and hold on for dear life.

"Sit with me during the ceremony. I'll save a seat for you."

I don't know what makes me say it, given my stated position on weddings. And the fact that we're not seventh graders making cafeteria seating plans for lunch period. I also don't know why I feel as though I'm down on one knee waiting for a response that will change my life forever. It's such a stupid request. I'm not a senti-mental person. I just had this vision of, I don't know, the two of us being together during an important moment. Maybe holding hands. Maybe dancing together later.

Bullshit, all of it.

You'd think I'd know better by now.

"I can't," she says, already moving away and pulling her arm free as she issues this latest in a long line of rejections. I *think* I see regret in her eyes, but I'm sure the record will reflect by now that I'm not great at deci-phering her body language. And maybe I'm mistaking that for straight deer in headlights because she's wondering what she has to do to escape me and my endless overtures. "I have to stay with Ella. Make sure she looks okay for the pictures."

Foolish down to the marrow of my bones, I can't let it go. "Later, then—"

"I'm sorry," she says, hurrying out.

I follow her after a beat or two, determined to arrange my features into something that looks happy and get my sister down the aisle. But my face feels crooked. And my chest still feels as though it's got that same old hole in it. Although, in fairness, the hole seems to be getting bigger.

She's *sorry*.

Huh. Yeah. Sure.

I'm sorry.

Mia?

She couldn't care less how many times she kicks me in the teeth when I stick my neck out for her.

I SNEAK away from the reception as early as I politely can, which is sometime after eleven, when the dancing kicks into full swing under the massive tent. If I'd had my way, I'd have left the Hamptons and headed back to the city as soon as I zipped Ella into her wedding gown. Actually, strike that. If I'd had my way, I'd have abandoned all remaining design responsibilities the second I realized that Liam was Ella's brother. Let someone else have the solemn responsibility of making sure that Ella gets zipped into her dress and keeps her train straight for the photos. I know we're friends now, but it's a new friendship. As such, you can only ask so much of a person. Asking me to peacefully coexist with Liam dives right across the line of asking too much.

It's not like his looming presence is conducive to me enjoying anything about this celebratory weekend.

It's not like I'm in the mood to see some other couple live happily ever after when my ongoing fear threatens to suffocate me, and Liam and I can't even manage to comfortably occupy the same room.

Which is a real shame, because the wedding was fabulous.

I kick off my heels as soon as I let myself into the peaceful semidarkness of my room. Then I sink onto the bench at the end of my bed, rest my elbows on my knees and drop my head into my hands, bracing for the wave of despair that I know is coming.

In the entire world, there's nothing like seeing happy couples and ecstatically smiling faces in every direction to make you feel lost and alone. I feel as though someone unscrewed my head from my neck and packed me full of misery from top to bottom. I can't breathe with the misery. Literally cannot breathe. And don't get me started on my emotional exhaustion.

I sit up straight and rub my chest in a doomed attempt to get my lungs to loosen up. It doesn't help. I don't think anything short of a lobotomy will rescue me from this wretched existence, where I'm incapable of thinking about anything other than Liam and yet *still* can't figure out what to do about him.

Does that make sense? I think not.

Luckily, my room is stocked with alcohol in the cabinet. All the way across the room. I heave myself to my feet with a resigned sigh —

"What's wrong, Starlight?" comes Liam's voice from the armchair in the corner.

Oh, God.

I jump and emit an undignified squawk as I take a closer look. The hard planes of his face are partially illuminated by the lamp on the table next to him. The top couple buttons of his shirt are undone. His black tie dangles on either side of his collar.

His expression? Flat but unyielding. Dangerous

enough to produce a trail of foreboding down my spine.

"What the hell are you doing lurking in my room?"

"I'm not lurking. I'm sitting in plain sight. You were thinking too hard to notice me. I can hear the gears clanking in your brain all the way over here."

"It's been a long day. I'm tired. I don't have the energy for another go-round with you."

"Why not?" he says. "Aren't you *energized* by that beautiful wedding? Aren't you *thrilled* to be surrounded by so many happy couples who found their soul mates? You women are big on that, aren't you? *Soul mates?* Doesn't it give you hope to know it's possible to live happily ever after?"

Something about the S-word coming out of *his* mouth while he's sitting, uninvited, in *my* room really pisses me off. And don't get me started on his taunting tone or the glint of defiance in his eyes.

"Look at you. Learning big new words and using them correctly in a sentence. Who'd have thought?"

"I'm full of surprises," he says with a crooked smile. "I hate weddings, in case you're interested. Not that you're interested in anything about me that's not directly attached to my dick."

I wince inwardly, working hard to keep my dismay off my face. I can't let one drop of blood fall in these shark-infested waters.

I could almost laugh. If only he knew how interested in him I am. Guess I'm a better actress than I gave myself credit for.

"Weddings make me sad," he continues. "The loneliest place in the world is a wedding reception. Nothing like it for making you realize what a shit show your life is."

"Fascinating. I'm sure that made you a ball of laughs at dinner tonight."

"You have no idea. But that's no reason to ruin my sister's big night just because I'm in a shitty mood."

"Aren't *you* the soul of consideration? Too bad you didn't apply that to me when it came to letting yourself into my room uninvited."

"True. The thing is, I know what's wrong with *me* tonight. But what's on *your* mind that makes *you* look so sad on such a great night?"

"Nothing," I say, way too quickly. "Like I said, I'm tired."

"Nothing." He raises a tumbler, toasts me and gulps down something amber, exposing the strong column of his throat. "Why am I not surprised?"

There's no answering the question, so I don't even try. Right now seems like a good time to stick to offense.

"Why are you in my room, Liam? It's late."

"I told you." He levels all that dark intensity straight at me. The feeling is deeply unsettling. Like rounding a bend on a hiking trail and discovering the unblinking eyes and crouched body of a cougar lying in wait. "We need to talk. And I figured you wouldn't have the guts to come to me, so I came looking for you. Like I said I would. You didn't forget, did you?"

I didn't forget. I just foolishly allowed myself to be lured into a false sense of security when he didn't approach me all night. He didn't speak to me. Didn't try to sit by me at dinner or commandeer me on the dance floor. Hell, I don't even think he looked at me all night. And I should know, because I was busy shooting surreptitious glances in *his* direction the whole time. I thought he'd decided to let me off the hook for now. I even felt a tiny stab of disappointment that he decided to throw a little mercy my way.

I should have known better.

"Like I keep saying, it's late and I'm tired. Just because *you* decide *you're* ready for some big talk doesn't mean the time is right."

"I disagree."

We watch each other warily, stalemated.

"Are you drunk?" I ask, battling that growing feeling of unease.

"No." He studies his glass, which is nearly empty now. "The idea has some appeal, but it seems important for me to be sober tonight."

I don't like the sound of that. I don't like the sound of that at all.

I think hard, eager to do anything I can to slow this runaway train down before it jumps the tracks and blows some shit up around here. He got such a funny look on his face earlier when I refused to sit by him during the ceremony. Maybe I hurt his feelings. Maybe I should start there. Or with his remarks at the reception. He was delightful. The soul of charm and wit. George Clooney couldn't have done any better.

"You did a great job on your speech, by the way," I say.

"Oh?"

"Ella and Ryker were really touched. I could tell."

"Ah."

His indifference couldn't be more absolute. We might as well be discussing fiscal policies in Luxembourg.

"And I, ah, wanted to tell you I'm sorry," I continue.

A spark of interest as he cocks his head. "For?"

"I didn't mean to hurt your feelings about not sitting

by you during the ceremony."

A flicker of amusement. *"That's* what you want to apologize for?"

"I just think we need to stick to the physical part of our relationship without muddying the waters."

His expression flatlines, his brows lowering until I can barely see his glinting eyes. Which might be a blessing.

"So…fucking only?" he asks. "That's our arrangement?"

I don't know what it is, but something about hearing it in such crass terms makes me cringe.

"That's the part we're good at." I can't quite hide my regret. Or my bitterness. Or my fear that my growing obsession with him will take over my entire life the way it did before. "The rest does too much damage."

"The rest is *eating me alive*. And I really wish you gave two shits about that. Or thought twice about rejecting me every fucking time I reach out to you."

His voice and his expression descend into anguish at the end, catching me by surprise. I never like to get too close to the idea that he's suffering as much as I am. I don't know what to do with that concept.

"Liam."

"I've spent my entire adult life trying to get my shit together, Mia. Are you aware of that? I've had a partying phase. A med-school phase." Humorless laugh. "I've been with more women than I care to remember. I watched my mother die. I reconnected with my sister, which is great. A huge surprise. You think I ever thought she'd ask me to give her away at her wedding? Family means something in my life now. Something *good*. Her husband told me he considers me his brother now. And he acts like he means it. I've never had a *brother*. You know what that means to me?"

"Of course I do," I say, thinking of all the holidays he spent with me and my family because he couldn't handle spending the time with his passive-aggressive mother and her list of grievances. "I'm happy for you."

"I've had all my medical training," he says, ticking points off on his fingers. "I've tried to become a great doctor, which is what I thought I wanted my whole life. I developed a little gadget that should save millions of lives, and I made a fortune doing it. Hell, I've done it all. This is me succeeding in life. Except for one thing. The big thing. *You*."

I don't open my mouth. I don't dare.

"Thanks to *you*, I still have a giant fucking hole inside me." He thumps his chest. "I'm still here late at night trying to get you to give me the time of day. So, yeah, I need to get past this. And I'm betting you do too."

"Obviously, you're not going to let this drop," I say briskly. I cannot begin to tell you the effort it requires for me to keep my expression neutral and my voice crisp and steady when my throat feels so tight and I have the sensation that an earthquake is brewing inside me. "Why don't we grab coffee tomorrow after we've had a good night's sleep—"

His face twists as he snarls at me. *Snarls*.

"It's been twelve fucking years, Mia! We've waited long enough!"

His voice booms off the walls, startling me and shattering my self-control.

"This is not all about *you*!" I shout.

"Damn straight." Just like that, he's calm again. If you don't look too closely at the wild light in his eyes.

"It's all about *both* of us. And having this discussion on a wedding day feels right. Even if it's not *our* wedding day. Even if we never had *our* wedding day."

Our wedding day.

I hate him for breaking our unspoken rule and saying it out loud. Ridiculous, I know, but you won't catch the magical community in the Harry Potter books saying Voldemort's name aloud either, will you?

Some things provoke too much fear and heartache. Some topics must be avoided at all costs.

"I'm not doing this now," I say. "Not with all this anger. I'm not dealing with you like this."

"Why not?" He stares me dead in the face, his expression cold. Heartless. "You made me like this. So that means you earned it."

I cock my head, certain I'm mishearing.

"*I* earned it?" The accusation is so stunning—so outrageous—that I could shriek with fury. I could smash something. I could hit him. But the one thing I must never do is lose control and let him know how badly he's hurt me. So I rein in all that dark emotion, head for the door and swing it open, keeping my hand on the knob. "Get. The. Fuck. Out."

He shrugs with what looks like complete indifference, gets up, comes my way, hands deep in his pockets. I feel an overwhelming surge of relief. For exactly two seconds. Until, with another snarl, he wrenches the door out of my hand and slams it shut.

"I don't think so, Starlight," he says, snatching my hand and forcing something into it. I'm stunned to see that it's a beautiful diamond ring with a halo. Once upon a time, it was *my* ring. "Not until you tell me why you broke our engagement and ripped my guts out."

12

MIA

AND THERE IT IS. His grievance against me. Unforgotten and unforgiven.

I'm surprised we've managed to dance around it for this long, even given my best efforts to not discuss it. But I'm more surprised by how much of a relief it is to get it out there in the open, painful as it is.

Meanwhile, the beautiful ring sits in my palm, unnaturally hot and heavy. As though it's got unholy powers like the One Ring from Lord of the Rings. Hell, maybe it does. God knows everything the ring symbolized between me and Liam has ruled my life for the last umpteen years.

"There was no need for us to get married anymore," I tell him, working hard to keep my spine straight and my knees tremble-free as I close my fingers around the ring and walk a few steps away to open up some space between us. "You know that."

His eyes narrow. "No...*need*? Is that what you just said?"

"Why are you looking at me like that? You were there when we had this discussion."

"I didn't understand it then, and I'm trying to understand it now, so maybe you can humor me. I'm dying to hear your take on things. In case I missed something. Since we're finally talking and all."

I take a deep breath with no idea where to start. Especially with all these minefields in every direction.

"You know this, Liam. I got pregnant—"

"*We* got pregnant. Since *I* was the one charged with working the condoms." Chilling smile from Liam. "And did a shitty job of it, by all accounts."

I blink. He doesn't blame himself for that, does he?

"Yeah, well, we wouldn't have even needed the condoms if I hadn't had that sinus infection. But the antibiotics made my pills ineffective. And what difference does it make at this late date? I don't blame you for what happened."

"Sure you do. And I blame myself for not being more careful."

"Accidents happen, Liam."

"I didn't expect them to happen to *us*," he says.

The back of my mouth fills with the bitter taste of resentment.

"I see. That must be why you said—what was it? I want to make sure I get this right—*What the fuck are we going to do now?* and couldn't even look at me when I told you I was pregnant."

"I was surprised."

"Clearly. Whereas getting pregnant when *I'd* landed a job in Milan after graduation and *you'd* gotten into Harvard Med was all part of *my* devious master plan."

"*I* was surprised. *You* were surprised. We needed to

let things settle and figure out what to do with ourselves. Which we did."

"We had no business talking about getting married. We were way too young."

"That must be why I proposed and you said *yes*," he says, his jaw so tight he can barely get the words out.

"Oh, come on," I say, tired of this wounded act. "You didn't really want to get married. You were just trying to do your naïve twenty-two-year-old version of the right thing."

His eyes flash murder at me. "So this is all a joke to you now? Or was it all a joke to you then?"

"It was never a joke," I say, stung. "It was a beautiful idea. I was grateful that you wanted to marry me."

"Grateful?" he says, his voice deathly quiet.

"It was a beautiful idea, but it was a bad plan. Where did we think we would live?"

"In Cambridge," he says without missing a beat. "In student housing or an apartment."

"How would you get through med school with a little kid running around underfoot?"

"It's been done before. We would have managed."

"And how would I have launched my design career from Cambridge? Maybe I'm crazy, but I'm pretty sure it's not exactly one of the design capitals of the world."

"No idea," he says, shrugging. "But I would have been happy to talk about it and figure something out if you'd given us half a chance."

"I gave us half a chance," I say. "Anyway, it's all water under the bridge. I had a miscarriage. We dodged a bullet. Problem solved."

I'm regretting my poor choice of words even before I see him recoil.

"I didn't see the loss of our kid as the solution to any problem," he says.

"You know what I mean," I quickly say. "That was a bad way to put it. But don't act like it wasn't a relief on some level. Don't act like you wanted to get married."

"No. Don't *you* act like you know what *I* wanted. Don't act like *you* ever took my proposal seriously."

His vehemence throws me off guard. "Why are you saying that, Liam? You know how much I loved you."

Whoa. Wrong thing to say.

He charges forward, getting right in my face and leveling all that anger at me like a shotgun blast.

"I don't want to hear that bullshit from you!"

"It's not bullshit!"

"Sure it is, Starlight. You couldn't get out of there fast enough once you lost the baby. You couldn't *wait* to take that ring off your finger and give it back. Why not own it? We're supposed to be clearing the air here, right? Let's clear it. Why not admit you chose your career over a life with me?"

"What are you talking about?"

"Cut the drama. You *wanted* to go to Milan. You *wanted* to be a big designer. That was way more important to you than any commitment you made to *me*. You put me and our relationship in your rearview mirror so fast it made my head spin. You didn't think twice about it or me once the baby was gone. Hell, I'm surprised you remembered my name after all this time. Why not admit it? Get it off your chest."

These allegations are so unfounded and unfair that absolute stupefaction locks me down tight.

I realize, with some detachment, that my hands are

trembling. I work hard to get my words together and bring some accuracy to the proceedings.

"There's nothing to admit other than we were both young and scared and we had no business throwing around lifelong concepts like marriage and children. That's like a toddler playing with a lighter. Something bad's going to happen. Something permanent. Without a baby, there was no reason to get married. Or to talk about marriage. Not when we still had so much to do with our careers."

"Nope. No reason at all. It wasn't like we loved each other and wanted to spend our lives together. Well, one of us did, but it takes two to tango."

"It takes two to tango, but why would *I* have been the one doing all the sacrificing in your little happily-ever-after scenario?" I say. "Why was *I* supposed to give up my career dreams so *I* could freeze my ass off in Cambridge raising a baby by myself while *you* spent every waking moment on your training to became a doctor? Did you think of that?"

A *gotcha* gleam appears in his eyes, making my heart seize up.

"Actually, I *did* think of that," he says silkily. "I *didn't* think it was fair for you to do all the sacrificing. That's why I reached out to NYU and Columbia. You remember that I also got into NYU and Columbia, don't you? Sorry, that's an unfair question, since you never gave a damn about me. I can't expect you to remember little details like that. Anyway, I reached out to both admissions departments."

All the wind whooshes out of my sails. Just like that. This news actually makes me feel lightheaded. My brain tries to process this information while I gape at him, but the pieces of this story don't fit together. Meaning that I'm going to need a hell of a lot more explaining. He can't just pull the pin and lob a grenade like that into my life.

"You did *what*?" I ask, my voice barely audible.

"I wanted to see about, I don't know, transferring to one of them after a year at Harvard Med. I figured once the baby was born, you could find a job at some fashion house in the city. Call me crazy, but NYC *is* one of the fashion capitals of the world, right? I thought it was a workable plan for us to be together because we loved each other and we had a baby on the way, but then the baby died and you couldn't be done with me fast enough. *I* was trying to figure out how we could be together, and *you* had one foot out the door. Guess you could say we weren't exactly on the same page. Ah, well. What can you do? C'est la vie."

A sudden wave of dizziness hits, making the room swim out of focus.

This can't be true. My entire life can't turn on this flimsy dime.

"Why...why didn't you tell me any of this before? We could have talked about this."

"*You* could have given me a chance. If you'd loved me half as much as I loved you. 'Cause, see, *I* was already trying to figure out how we could be together. Even *before* you turned up pregnant. *I* was already trying to figure out how to broach the subject with you. Get my courage up. Ask if you'd think about finding a job here in the States. I actually went so far as to check out med schools in Italy. See if *that* would be a possibility. I didn't want us to be three thousand miles apart. So I was *thrilled* about a baby. *Thrilled* I had an excuse to make us into a permanent family. *Thrilled* to find a ring and propose. *Thrilled* when you said *yes*. But hey. That was just me. Clearly."

I stare down at the beautiful ring I proudly wore for the entire six days of our engagement, hot tears clouding my vision as I remember every single detail about his proposal. Like the radiant happiness on his face as he dropped to one knee. My own soaring giddiness. Our fevered kisses. The way he slid the ring onto my trembling finger, a perfect fit. An exquisite promise of our future together as partners and lovers.

The memories crowd inside me, mingling with my misery and leaving no room for my breath. A hot tear or two splashes down my cheek, unstoppable as I think about all of the might-have-beens and what-ifs. Would I have married him if I hadn't lost the baby? Yes. Would I have married him without the baby? Not yet. But would I have happily stayed here in the U.S. with him, setting up housekeeping in the city while I launched my design career and he went to med school? Falling asleep with him and waking up with him? Laughing with him? Loving him?

A thousand times *yes*.

Would we have lived happily ever after? I don't know. We were young and immature no matter how you slice it.

But...

I can't shake the feeling that we would have been a hell of a lot better off, even if the relationship had died a natural death, than we are now with all the wasted time and regrets.

And that's a bitter pill to choke down. Take it from me.

"What's wrong?" His jeering voice sounds as though

it belongs in the stands of some high-stakes NFL playoff game as the opposing team's player lines up for a kick. "Cat got your tongue? Am I missing something? Did I hear you wrong when you said we'd be crazy to get married anyway?"

Several more tears fall. There's no stopping them now.

"I wish you'd told me this before, Liam."

"I did!"

"Not the part about transferring to a med school in the city."

"What was I supposed to do? Beg you not to leave when you were busy throwing my ring back in my face? Get down on my knees for you *again*? Steal your suitcase and hide it so you couldn't pack for Milan?"

Oh, God. He's right.

I remember the proud young man he was back then. I juxtapose the buoyant happiness in his eyes when I said *yes* versus the dawning misery when I ended the engagement...

I feel sick.

On top of that, a sudden wave of exhaustion kicks in. I cover my face with my hands and hide there for a second or two. I watch the train wreck play out in my mind—over and over again—and wish I had a magic wand so I could go back and undo it all.

I finally raise my head again and somehow meet his accusatory gaze.

"Don't pretend you're sad about the whole thing," he says, his presence growing steadily more imposing the angrier he gets. "Your acting skills aren't that great. Hate to tell you."

How did we get this far into this painful conversation

without me making myself any clearer? How do I make him understand? How can I say it? What words should I use?

"I thought I was doing the right thing," I say. "I didn't see how we could get married and still achieve our goals."

His scowl deepens, telling me I've screwed it up yet again.

"Oh, okay. I get it," he says, his voice growing steadily louder. "So your *yes* was a provisional yes. *That's* the issue here. *That's* the disconnect I didn't appreciate. When *I* proposed, I wanted you to be my *wife*. For the rest of my life. Come hell or high water. No matter what. But when *you* said yes, you were only agreeing to a legal baby daddy. Isn't that right, Starlight? Makes. Perfect. Sense."

"No, that's *not* right!" I cry. "I didn't want you to resent me one day —"

"Well, *that* worked out beautifully."

" —and I wanted you to be happy!"

"I *was* happy!" he roars, anger twisting his features into a funhouse mirror version of his face. "In my entire life, I've never been as happy as I was with *you*! I *loved* you!"

"I loved you too!"

"I would've done *anything* for you! *Anything* to be with you! That's why it meant something when I asked you to be my wife! And you *ruined* it! Everything in my life since then has been in reaction to what happened between us! When I'm not remembering you, I'm trying to recapture what we had with someone else! Do you get that I've still got you stuck in the middle of my life? Do you care?"

I blink, then go very still while I replay that whole bit back. The words resonate through me as though someone has rung a gong inside my brain. I frown and concentrate, determined to run through them again and make sure I really heard what I just heard.

I open my mouth, but my voice is operating on a delay.

"*I* ruined it?"

"Don't deny it!"

"*Recapture what we had*? Is *that* what you were trying to do when you fucked Janet right under my nose to punish me?"

He stiffens, his steely defiance wavering. I wait while the gears clank and grind in his twisted male thought process, dying to hear what he comes up with.

Nothing good, I'll bet. Matter of fact, I'd stake money on it.

Because this is the thing about Liam. Right here. He talks a good game. No one does soulful eyes better than he does. (Side note: no one is better at falling for his act than *I* am.) He's great at shining the spotlight on *me* and all *my* transgressions. But when the time comes to examine all the ways *he* pissed in our swimming pool, he goes mute. He can't find the words.

His sudden silence after reading *me* the riot act for all *my* wrongdoing generates a volcanic level of fury inside me. I feel it in the scorching heat that climbs my neck and crawls over my face.

"Don't tell me you forgot about *that* part of our history!" I shout, beyond caring if anyone anywhere in this lovely house on this special night hears me. "You're so busy talking about what *I* did! Let's talk about what *you* did!"

"It was a knee-jerk reaction, Mia," he says quietly, his shoulders drooping when he was so puffed-up and righteous not three seconds ago. "I did the exact wrong thing. But I fell apart after you broke our engagement."

"You *fell apart*," I say, my voice strangled by all the hypocrisy. "*Now* it makes perfect sense. It's *my* fault. *I* forced you to find comfort in some other woman's pussy. Got it. I'm sorry I did that to you. You poor thing."

"Mia." He steps closer, one hand outstretched as though he wants to touch me. I smack that hand away. I don't want it anywhere near me. "You left after you broke our engagement. I was upset. I went to the pub. I got drunk —"

"You called her. Don't forget that part."

His eyes roll closed. He stands there for a beat or two, silent as a forgotten grave. When his lids flick open again, he looks stricken. Ashamed.

I don't care. My heart is too hard.

"Answer me! While *I* was at home crying my eyes out because of the miscarriage and then crying them out some more because of the way you told me to get the fuck out when I said I didn't think we needed to get married, *you* were calling your little fuck buddy! Who was waiting in the wings the whole two years we were together! She couldn't *wait* to tell me she'd spent the night with you! So don't pretend you didn't call her!"

He swallows hard, making his Adam's apple bob. A muscle pulses in his temple.

"I called her, yeah."

The admission only fuels my anger. I swipe away my hot tears, as infuriated with myself as I am with him.

"I was *such* a little fool," I say. "I thought that was the worst night of my life. I cried and wrote out a whole little speech in my head. About how I still loved you and how we could still make our relationship work because I wouldn't be in Milan forever. I was planning to wake up in the morning, find you and make *everything* right. Imagine how much worse the *next* night was when I found out that the whole time *I* was crying and pasting together a scheme to get you back, *you* were making yourself feel better by putting your dick in some other woman's mouth!"

"It wasn't like that, Mia," he says, reaching for me again.

But I hold my hands up and back away from all his fervent intensity because I've had enough. There's enough damage strewn between us to keep FEMA busy for years to come.

"You think *I* hurt *you*? *You* hurt *me*!" I let out a bark of laughter that has more than a tinge of hysteria in it. "*You* hurt *me*! And the whole episode just proves that I was right about us being too young to get married! So I don't want to hear any more of your victim bullshit about me breaking your heart and ruining our relationship. There's more than enough blame to go around here."

"WELL, well, well, if it isn't my favorite designer in all the world," says Ella's Aunt Gilda first thing Monday morning, as soon as I poke my head into Valentina's, her European bakery in Greenwich Village. I've caught her after the early rush when the place is relatively quiet, so she has time to come out from behind the counter and engulf me in a bear hug that feels surprisingly comforting to my jangled nerves. "What brings you down here? Did you come to soak up more praise for your beautiful creation the other day?"

"No, nothing like that," I say, laughing as she lets me go. I decide not to confess that, having gnawed my frozen Junior's cheesecake last night, I'm in desperate need of additional empty calories to consume while I continue obsessing about the Liam situation. "Ella brought me those Portuguese egg tarts every time she came in for a fitting. Now I'm spoiled and addicted. And probably fat soon, if I keep on my current trajectory."

"You? Never. You've got that natural tall and willowy

build. You're so gorgeous, I'm surprised you have any female friends. We're all jealous. What about coffee?"

"You're too kind. I'm going to need coffee. Plenty of cream and sugar. And a black coffee for my brother, please. He's meeting me here. He'll pick out his own pastry when he gets here."

"You got it, doll," she says, heading back behind the counter to get started on my order while I grab a seat at a table by the window.

"I'm surprised you didn't take a day or two off after the big weekend," I say.

"I wish. But with the remodel…I can't turn my back on those clowns for a *second*."

She flaps a hand toward a huge flap of plastic sheeting that covers the remnant of a wall that's been knocked down since I was here last. Things do seem to be bustling back there. Right on cue, the grizzled, grumpy and red-faced head of a man pokes through the flap.

"Hey! I can hear you back here!" he tells Aunt Gilda in an accent that's been heavily marinated in all things New York for generations back, unless I'm much mistaken. "You keep calling us *clowns*, I'm gonna order my guys to slow down. See how you like *that*."

"*You* slow down and *I'm* going to start rationing your afternoon snacks," she says serenely. "See how popular you are with your men when they stop getting their churros at three o'clock."

"Now you're just getting nasty," he mutters, disappearing back behind the flap.

She and I grin at each other. She winks.

"So how are things coming on the new addition?" I ask.

"Fine, as long as I crack some heads together at least once a day. Which is a good thing, because Ella's expanding into wedding cakes. You know this already. So when she and Ryker get back from Tahiti, she's going to have a full plate around here. I hope he's letting the poor woman get a little rest."

I raise my brows. "On their honeymoon?"

"Yeah, you're right," she says with a resigned sigh as she brings over the coffees and my tart. "Pipe dream — Oh, this must be your brother! Come in, come in, fine sir. Aren't you a handsome devil?"

I roll my eyes, but no one notices. Michael is too busy looking broody and intense, which is what he does with his tall, dark and handsome good looks, and Aunt Gilda is too busy looking dazed and dazzled.

"Michael Jamison," he tells her, extending a hand. "And you are…?"

"Gilda Arnold." She seems a bit breathless now. Let's just say it doesn't stretch my imagination to picture a younger Gilda slipping her phone number or hotel key into his pocket. But that's the standard female response to Michael, to be fair. "Owner of Valentina's."

"Pleasure. I've heard good things."

"I try never to disappoint a paying customer. What can I get you? I already brought coffee."

He glances at the display case. "Belgian waffle. Plain. Thanks."

"Be right back," she says, dashing off.

I won't be surprised if she returns with a spritz of perfume and refreshed lipstick.

"Hey," he says, leaning in for a kiss.

"Hey," I say glumly, letting my perky and polite social mask slip now that he's here. I'm running on fumes and need some serious advice before my churning thoughts cause me to spontaneously combust. No one knows me like he does, so I consider him my own personal cavalry riding to the rescue. "I'm glad you're here. Thanks for coming on such short notice."

"Anything for you. How'd it go?"

"The wedding was amazing."

"I mean with you and Liam."

I think that over, trying to find the exact right image. "You know how the Gulf Coast looks when a hurricane comes through?"

"Yep."

"It was the emotional version of that."

"Yikes," he says. "Why?"

I hesitate. "I know this goes without saying, but he's your best friend. I just want to make sure —"

"He's my best friend, but you're my sister. My loyalty is with *you*. I'd never break your confidence."

"Thanks," I say with a quick smile. "I needed to hear that."

Gilda reappears with his Belgian waffle, sees the lay of the land with our tight faces and makes a discreet and hasty retreat before we can thank her.

"So what's going on?" he asks when she's out of earshot again.

"We had it all out. It was ugly." My chin quivers as I remember everything we said. Everything I felt, most of which I still feel. Hurt. Anger. Most of all? Shock. "It was really ugly."

"Don't kill me," he says.

"Oh, God, what now?"

"I wasn't thrilled about my buddy the player hooking up with my twin sister. Initially. But you two worked.

You were a good team. I thought you had a chance of going the distance. What happened? Neither one of you ever said."

"He never told you?" I say, startled by this information.

"Nope. You both clammed up. You wouldn't talk about why you broke up. Hell, neither one of you mentioned the other one's name until recently. What could be so bad?"

Much as I need his advice, I belatedly realize that it's not that easy to open the door to all my darkest secrets when it's been locked and sealed this whole time. But there's something so reassuring about his steady gaze and reassuring presence that I feel some of my tension slipping away.

"I, ah...found out I was pregnant. Senior year. Right around graduation."

He freezes.

"Don't judge me," I snap. "Condoms don't always work."

"I'm not judging you. I'm thinking that there but for the grace of God go I. So what happened?"

I double-check him for sincerity before continuing, mollified.

"Liam proposed." I slip my hand into my pocket, where I've been carrying the ring ever since he gave it back to me the other night, and finger the smooth band. Something about it feels oddly reassuring, like bumping into an old friend. "I said yes. I had a miscarriage a few days later. I told him we didn't need to get married after all. He responded by getting drunk and sleeping with Janet. Who called me and gleefully told me about it."

"*Christ.*"

"Exactly. So that was that. He went off to Harvard Med. I went off to Milan. The end. Until now. We've kind of danced around all these issues, but we really got into it after the wedding the other night."

"And…?"

"Let's just say that peace has not been restored in the kingdom," I say glumly.

"Because…?"

"Because we both still have poisonous levels of hard feelings. Because we both think that the other person was the villain."

"Not sure one conversation is enough to work through all of that," he says, shrugging. "Sleep on it. Let it marinate. See how you feel."

I blink and stare down at the table, letting the idea take hold.

He's right, of course. He usually is. That's why I keep him around.

"I didn't think we were ready to get married right out of college," I say.

Another shrug. "Some people aren't. Some people are. And they make it work."

Something about the way he says that catches my attention. I frown at him. "You think *we* were ready?"

"Only you can answer that."

"Well, what are you saying?" I say, frustration making my voice pitch higher. "If you've got some answers here, now's the time for you to start sharing them."

"No answers here, but I have an opinion. Which is that Liam didn't have to ask you to marry him if he didn't want to. He came from money. Unmarried people have kids all the time. They write each other checks for child support. Easy. No matrimony necessary."

"Yeah, but maybe he just wanted to do the noble thing," I say, running various scenarios through my mind. Maybe I'll latch on to something that makes sense if I brainstorm long enough. "Or maybe he wanted to make sure that his kid didn't grow up like Ella did, with a father who didn't have an official place in her life."

He gives me a pitying look. "Why keep putting yourself through all these mental gymnastics? Why not consider the possibility that he loved you and wanted to marry you for *you*?"

The idea makes my heart ache so hard that I rub my chest.

"Because then I'd have to reevaluate how I feel about the whole situation. And I don't want to do that. It's easier to think I have the righteous hand of God on my side."

"I see," he says with a tinge of amusement.

"You're not honestly telling me you think Liam was ready to get married back then. Come on. He couldn't even keep his pants on for ten minutes when I said I didn't want to get married. He proposed, but he didn't really mean it. You and I both know that."

"Those are two separate issues. Would it have worked? Maybe not. It's a pretty hard commute between Cambridge and Milan."

The memory of Liam's confession that he'd have transferred to a med school in the city for me makes my conscience squirm.

"But like I keep telling you," Michael continues, "if the issue is whether he meant it or not, the answer is hell yeah. He meant it."

I search my brother's implacable expression, desperate for answers. "How can you be so sure?"

He blows out a breath and runs his hands across the top of his head, ruffling his hair and clearly thinking hard.

"He won't appreciate me telling you this, Mia, but he spiraled for about a year after you left."

"*Spiraled?*" I say, my heart stopping cold.

"Let's just say that he had more than his fair share of partying and women. And that he almost got himself kicked out of med school."

"*What?*"

"You heard me."

I think about the Liam I knew back then. He liked to have fun, yeah, but he was a brilliant student. Naturally gifted but also hardworking. Never missed a class no matter how late we'd stayed up the night before, which is not something our entire friend group could say. From the second I met him until the present, Liam has always been obsessed with becoming the best possible doctor.

I think about how heartsick and lonely I felt after graduation and during my first few months in Milan. How slow I was to make friends. To go out. I think about all the nights I cried myself to sleep. All the times I picked up the phone to text or call him. All the weight I lost. All the despair. It was so easy to imagine him blithely going on with his life and never giving me a second thought.

But then I remember the other half of this equation. My heart hardens again.

"If he was so freaking heartbroken over me, then why did he turn to some other woman?" I demand.

"Speak on behalf of your whole miserable sex. Give me an explanation that makes sense."

"Impulsivity? Immaturity? Stupidity? All of that? None of that? How should I know? Didn't you ever do anything stupid back then?"

I snort. "Yeah. I fell in love with someone who broke my heart."

"Who hasn't? Why are you so special?"

I wince. Both because he's right but also because he's fresh off his divorce after a five-year marriage. It was uncontested and they had no children to divvy up, but still. If I had any empathy for the poor guy, I wouldn't be bugging him for romantic advice at this delicate juncture.

"Sorry," I say. "You don't want to hear me blather on about my messy life. How are *you* doing?"

"Fine."

"No, really," I say, exasperated.

"Fine."

He says it with zero inflection both times. I read it for what it is, which is a door slammed in my face.

"Well, let me know when you're ready to start dating again. I have five thousand single friends who'd *love* to hook up with you."

"It's under control," he says, a dull flush rising over his cheeks.

Hang on. What is *that*?

"What gives?" I say, reaching across the table to give him a shoulder nudge.

"Nothing I want to get into."

"Come *on*. I just spilled all my embarrassing guts to you."

He hesitates while something in his expression changes. Softens.

"There was…a woman. At work. There was…*something*." His gaze shifts out of focus as he tries to analyze some memory. "But I was married, so…"

"You had an affair!" I cried, scandalized at this sign of moral equivalence from my upstanding brother.

"Is that likely?"

"Yeah, you're right," I say, deflating. "But you're free now. You should find her."

"What a fascinating idea."

"Yeah, okay, jackass," I say, laughing.

"Let's wrap this up," he says, checking his watch.

"Yeah. Let's. So what your bottom line for me?"

He looks politely puzzled. "No bottom line. It's over. Let it go. You saw each other. You gave it another shot, but it didn't work out. Now you know. You can go on with your regularly scheduled lives and move past this. No harm, no foul."

"No harm, no foul?" I cry, annoyed by the suggestion that it's just that easy to recover from everything that's happened between me and Liam. As though Liam and I got our wires crossed about when we were supposed to meet for drinks and need to get over it instead of harboring silly grudges. "It's *not* that easy."

"Sure it is. You design your clothes and let him do his heart surgeries. There are eight million people in the city. You never have to lay eyes on each other again if you don't want to. Move on. Forget him."

"But I can't—" I blurt, then stop myself.

Not great, but better than what I started to say: *But I can't just forget Liam. If I could, I would have done it by now.*

"But *what*?" he asks, a disquieting and knowing gleam of something wise in his eyes.

"Nothing," I say hastily, looking away.

But it's too late. The damage has been done. Now I know what's in my heart.

Evidently, so does he.

"Don't give up, Mia," he says, leaning in. "You'll regret it if you do. I know you will. And I'd tell him the same thing in case you're wondering."

"I hate you," I say, working hard to stifle a smile. "You're playing three-dimensional chess and I'm playing checkers with three pieces missing."

"No, you don't hate me," he says, grinning. He gives me a goodbye kiss and grabs his waffle to go. "That's the best advice you've ever heard. And you know it."

14

LIAM

"CAN YOU CHECK ON MR. Baxter's bloodwork?" I ask one of the nurses when I swing by the desk on my way out of the cardiac ICU. "It should've been back by now. I'm grabbing a quick lunch. I'll be in the café if you need me."

"I'll see what I can do," he says, picking up the phone.

"Appreciate it."

I hit the wall plate and slide my stethoscope into the pocket of my lab coat as the doors slide open for me. This whole thing with Mia has killed most of my appetite for the last few days, but I wouldn't say *no* to a grilled cheese and maybe a chocolate chip cookie—if I can't have what I really want, which is a couple of gin and tonics and a do-over on our conversation the other day. I punch the elevator button and am in the middle of rolling my shoulders to release some of the lingering tension from this morning's surgery when my phone buzzes.

Scowling—I'm not sure why medical emergencies

always seemed to pop up when I'm on my way to bed or a meal—I fish it out of my pocket and check the display:

Caller unknown.

"This is Dr. Wilder," I say, repressing an aggrieved sigh.

"Hey."

Mia.

My heart stops dead, making me grateful for the fact that I'm inches away from a world-class cardiac center and therefore easily resuscitated if I keel over. Excitement and adrenaline course through me with the force and speed of water out of a firehose. Funny how your day can go from shitty to shitty but hopeful just like that.

"Hey."

"It's, ah, Mia," she says. "My brother gave me your number."

Silly girl. As if there's a chance in a billion that I wouldn't recognize her voice.

"I know and I don't care how you got it. I'm glad you called."

"You are?"

"Mia," I say, as exasperated with myself as I am with her. She wouldn't sound so surprised if I'd done a better job making my feelings clear. "At times like this, I think we don't know the first damn thing about each other."

"There's a lot of that going around," she says wryly. "That's why I stopped by."

"Stopped by?" I say, my heart starting up again with a vengeance and pounding its way toward cardiac arrest. "What do you mean?"

"I'm on the first floor. I was hoping you had a minute to—"

"Where?"

"In the atrium."

"On my way," I say, then hang up and dash into the arriving elevator before she can change her mind.

I find her waiting for me in a semi-secluded seating area overlooking the courtyard and fountain outside. Her face is downturned, her expression unreadable. But she's fiddling with something in her pocket. These tiny signs of nerves from the woman who's always tied me up in knots is like a shot of courage directly to my bloodstream.

She's nervous. I'm scared shitless. But we're in this thing together.

"Hi," I say, catching her by surprise.

She looks up, her eyes widening and her cheeks reddening as she sees me cloaked in all my medical glory. I'm not bragging or anything, but this happens to me all the time. Doctors under the age of fifty, with all their hair, a fit body and good teeth, command attention around here. I usually ignore it whenever women notice me when I'm on duty.

But *Mia's* attention makes me feel as though I threw a little something to prevent cancer in with the polio vaccine. A king-of-the-world-level ego boost. Immense pride. Even more gratitude that I managed to pull doctor-hood off despite my many youthful efforts to shoot myself in the foot.

Even better? The unexpected shyness of her gaze doesn't suggest that she came to threaten me with a restraining order if I don't leave her alone. Just like that, my day goes from shitty but hopeful to not too bad at all.

"Hi," she says. "So you're really a doctor, eh?"

"I'm really a doctor."

Dimples appear, bracketing her mouth. It's not a full

smile, but it's close enough to make me pretty damn happy.

"It looks good on you. Did I catch you at a bad time?"

"Nope. Perfect time."

I'm not sure what the protocol is here, but it probably doesn't include a hug and kiss. And the excruciatingly polite vibe here feels very fragile, as though a single wrong move will cause something crucial but invisible to shatter. So I sit in the chair opposite her little loveseat and wait, hoping for the best.

"Sorry about showing up out of the blue," she says. "I decided to take a chance and just come. While I had the courage."

"And how's your courage now?" I ask quietly.

She thinks that over. "Shaky. I used most of it up getting here."

"Yeah. Mine's MIA, in case you're wondering."

"That makes me feel better." Her eyes crinkle at the outer corners, making something swoop inside me. "Guess that makes me a horrible person."

"Horrible person. Huh. Yeah. Guess that's why I've been hung up on you all these years."

"I'm sure I resolved *that* problem once and for all the other night with my outbursts."

"Nah." Much as I want to hold her gaze, there's something far too raw about it. Something far too intimate. I can't figure out whether I'm more afraid of revealing or seeing. "You didn't."

There's a delicious pause.

"I should've come sooner," she says softly, leaning closer as though she wouldn't mind touching me. "I haven't been sleeping."

"Just so you know, you would've found me sitting on your doorstep when you got home tonight," I confess. "We needed a cooling-off period. But another twenty-four hours without seeing you would've been more than I could manage."

"Yeah? Are you hearing my voice in your head? Because I've been hearing yours."

"Do tell," I say, resting my elbows on my knees to ease closer.

She opens her mouth. Hesitates. Closes her mouth. Clears her throat. Tries again.

"I've been so angry at you for so long. For sleeping with Janet. For the way she threw it in my face. For breaking my heart."

"Mia…"

"My anger kind of blocked everything else out. The thing with her negated all the good things we ever had. And it made it easy for me to believe you never really wanted to marry me anyway, baby or not. But…the last couple of days I've been thinking about how you said that *I* broke your *heart*. As opposed to me just, I don't know, pinching your ego by breaking off the engagement."

"I've got a big ego. Not going to lie. It's tough. But my *heart*?" I shrug.

She mirrors my posture and leans in, coming close enough for me to see the spikes of black and white through the blue irises. Close enough for me to see the honeyed dusting of freckles across her cheeks.

My restless hands want to reach for hers. To cling to her and make sure we don't slip up and lose this newfound connection.

I don't dare.

"It's hard now to remember exactly what I said when I told you I wasn't ready to get married," she says quietly. "What words I used. The tone of my voice. I keep running through it over and over and trying to figure out how I screwed up that one conversation so badly."

"What do you mean?"

"Because in my mind, I wasn't saying *no* to marriage. I was saying *not yet*." She stares me in the face, her eyes and expression beaming honesty straight at me, and plenty of it. "I wasn't saying goodbye to you. That wasn't my intention. That would've never been my intention. Because I was crazy in love with you and I couldn't imagine my life without you."

Couldn't?

Or *can't*?

I'm desperate to ask those questions, but, once again, I don't dare. I'm too afraid of saying or doing something that shuts her down and stops her from spilling these precious secrets.

"And…" She ducks her head, looking embarrassed now. "It's such a dumb question, but I have to ask. Why her? What did she have that I couldn't give you?"

"Nothing," I say, wishing I could identify the poisonous, self-destructive impulse that sent me to the pub that night when I should've kept my ass home and tried to work things out with Mia. What fool goes out shopping for plastic beads when he's got a flawless ten-carat diamond sitting on his kitchen table back home? Where's the sense? Where's the logic? "I can't explain it so that it makes sense to you. It doesn't make sense to me. I acted angry. I know I did. But really, I was hurt that you didn't love me the way I loved you. I felt like half a man. And I was reeling from having it all one day—baby, fiancée and clear path to a great future—and losing it all the next day."

"Exactly," she says sadly. "It still makes my head spin when I think about it. Did you ever think that maybe our relationship wasn't that great? Because look how easily it all fell apart."

"Not at all. It *was* great. We should have been more careful with it. Should've recognized how precious it was instead of feeling young and invincible. Like you said, I couldn't figure out how things went south so quickly. What did I say? What did I do? And instead of doubling down with you and trying to fix our relationship, I did the knee-jerk thing. Which was reach out to someone who wouldn't reject me. Who'd look at me like I was something special."

"I always thought you were something special, Liam. You *know* that."

I think that over.

"Maybe I did. Maybe it was easier to just focus on being angry at you and lashing out. Hell, I don't know. The only thing I know is that I regret it." Sudden ferocity makes my throat burn and my nostrils flare. Now is not the time or place for me to lose it, but my eyes feel hot and the tears are right there. "It's the worst mistake of my life. I wanted to lash out at you, but I hurt myself just as bad. And for what? She didn't mean anything to me. She never did. Never could. I hurt you. Hurt her. Hurt myself. Couldn't have done more damage if I'd tried."

She nods thoughtfully.

"The other night, you said something about consoling myself with another woman while you were hurting," I continue. "But there was no consolation. Not really. There was a temporary physical release that only made me feel worse about myself. More ashamed. Guiltier. It was a vicious cycle." I shake my head, disgusted even now.

"But you saw her again after that," she says stubbornly. "Once I went to Milan. I know you did. We have mutual friends who mentioned it to me."

I hang my head. What else can I do with this kind of shame weighing me down?

"I did, yeah," I confess. "I was with her and a lot of other women. Anything to keep my mind off you and what I'd thrown away. I was in self-destruct mode."

"What snapped you out of it?" she asks, looking troubled.

"Hell if I know. I think I got sick of myself. And then I got busy with med school. That saved me. Beyond that? The grace of God, I guess."

She nods, her unfocused gaze drifting off across the atrium.

"I should go," she says after a pause, reaching for her purse. "I didn't mean to take up so much of your time while you're at work."

Wait, *what*?

"Not yet," I quickly say. "I'm not sure where we stand."

Rueful smile from Mia. "Neither am I."

"Are we turning a page?" I ask. "Starting to forgive each other?"

"I'm not sure we should," she says gravely. "What will I focus my entire life around if I no longer hate you?"

That's easy.

"Loving me," I say.

"Yeah?" she says, her attention dipping to my mouth. "You think I can remember how?"

"I'm hoping you never stopped. That way you won't have to remember."

"Liam—"

"Shh," I say, praying none of my colleagues or patients are nearby as I cup her velvety cheek and zero in on her mouth.

She's right there with me, bringing that sultry scent of flowers with her and offering up her lips with a helpless sigh. A tiny coo of pleasure. And just like that, my day goes from not too bad at all to pretty freaking spectacular.

"I think we're starting to get on the right track here," I say when I let her up for air.

"Wouldn't *that* be a refreshing change?" she says, her cheeks rosy and her eyes shining. "So what now?"

"Now we work on not blowing it. Doing some more talking without bloodshed. Getting to know each other again. How does that sound?"

For a second, I think that she's going to say it sounds perfect, but then a shadow crosses her face. She shakes her head and tries to wave it off, but I'm not having it. If there's an obstacle here I want to know about it so I can blow that MF'er out of the water.

"Mia. What is it?"

Her search for the right words takes a second or two.

"I just…" She hesitates again, the color in her cheeks deepening. "I feel very fragile with you. It kills me to admit that, but I do. Be careful with me."

"I will," I say. The easiest and most heartfelt promise I ever made.

The woman has a better chance of being struck by lightning while on her way to cash in her winning lotto ticket than she does of me screwing things up again and letting her slip through my fingers a second time.

"As long as you're careful with me," I add.

"I'll see what I can do," she says, working hard to suppress her smile.

From there, it's easy enough to lean in for another kiss. A nuzzle or two.

"Stop trying to seduce me at my place of employment," I say after a final peck on her cheek. "Are you trying to get me in trouble? What will I do for money if you get me fired?"

That's when something miraculous happens.

She bursts into the kind of glorious and addictive laughter I remember so well from our time together. Sparkling eyes. Crinkled nose. Dimples. Head leaned back. All of that.

That laughter thrills and excites me. Restores me. Leaves my pulse thundering and my head spinning with one persistent thought.

I fucking love this woman.

15

"HEY," I say when Liam opens his apartment door for me a couple of nights later. He's wearing jeans and a white button-down shirt with the tails untucked and his sleeves rolled up. Sexy casual. "Why'd you have me come up? I could've waited in the lobby while you change your clothes. I thought we were having dinner?"

"We *are* having dinner," he says, looking amused as he swings the door wider to let me in before drying his hands on a kitchen towel. "Right here."

A vague flare of alarm flickers to life inside me, as though he's found some hidden knob in the vicinity of my rib cage and turned the flame on low. This whole date thing has me seriously off-kilter and discombobulated. As a confirmed control freak, let me assure you that I have absolutely no idea what to do with these feelings. I've been a bundle of nerves. All day. I had no idea what to wear. No idea what he expects to happen or not happen tonight. No inkling what to say to him now that we've officially decided we don't hate each other and are trying to build something here. I can make charming small talk when required, but only in fifteen-minute increments with a cocktail in one hand and a chicken kebab or other finger food in the other hand. I haven't had a successful date in over a year.

I'm not exaggerating when I tell you that I'm scared shitless. In this era of online dating, where the men I've come across lately seem to think that being on time is not a precursor to a positive experience with a new person but sending an unsolicited dick pic *is*, most evenings are doomed to failure even before I slide on my heels.

Tonight, the stakes feel unreasonably high. As though someone had the brilliant idea of seeing which two NASCAR drivers can deliver their favorite quarterbacks to the stadium first to determine which NFL teams get to play in the Super Bowl.

There's a lot of room for error here. A lot of ways this whole thing could go south on me and blow up in my face.

And yet I'm *so* excited. That's the worst thing about all this. I've been living for this moment. For the last couple of days, yeah, but also for the last umpteen years. I'm so thrilled to see him again after our breakthrough at the hospital. So hopeful about our future, delusional as that may be.

Honestly, this whole freaking date idea is fraught with peril.

It can only end with disaster and a gastric ulcer.

"Here?" I ask, warily peering past his shoulder and trying to see what he's got in store for me inside his swanky apartment, from which emanates the savory scent of sautéed onions and butter. If only the local branch of the FBI could send a team over to do a room-by-room sweep and let me know if the place is clear or

not. "You said we were getting dinner. As in, at a restaurant."

"I said no such thing," he says, slinging the towel over his shoulder. "I said, *Let's do dinner*. There's a difference. Are you coming in?"

"So…you ordered something in?" I say, staying right where I am.

"I cooked."

"Get the hell out of here," I say with a disbelieving laugh as I remember some of his catastrophic efforts in the kitchen back when we were together. Like the time I sliced my tongue on the bit of shell in the runny scrambled eggs he made for breakfast. Let's just say they were made with love but no skill. "You don't cook. I've got the PTSD to prove it. And I'm not eating ramen noodles unless they come from a Japanese restaurant around the corner."

"I cook now," he says proudly. "I want to impress you with my skillz. With a Z. I've acquired a few new tricks over the years. Come in and see."

My heart melts. Not that it hasn't already melted a million times over for this man, mind you.

"You can't just go cooking for me." I can't tell you how touched I am that he went to this kind of effort to make a good impression tonight. As if his credentials as a billionaire heart surgeon and the only man I've ever really loved don't swing the needle in his direction at all. "You didn't warn me or anything. I could have brought dessert or some wine. Now I'm empty-handed like the one rude asshole who always shows up at dinner parties."

"Don't worry. You're on cleanup duty. I'll make an extra mess to make sure you have a meaningful contribution to the dinner effort. Maybe smear sauce on the walls. Anything else?"

"No more surprises," I say, pointing at his nose as I head into the foyer, stow my umbrella by the door and slip out of my raincoat.

"I do what I want." His breath catches behind me as he shuts the door and takes my raincoat. "Holy shit. You look *amazing*."

"What, this little thing?" My face heats with pleasure as I make a show of adjusting the cap sleeves on my stretchy dress, which scoops low in the front and lower in the back. "You like it?"

"*Love* it. You make that?"

"I did. Speaking of sexy—"

"I don't believe I used the word *sexy*," he says, working hard to suppress a smile as he hangs up my things.

"You're right. Forget everything I was about to say about you and your lab coat the other day."

"Let's not be hasty," he says.

"Too late, Brad Pitt," I say, laughing and trying to hurry off as he reaches for me.

But I'm not fast enough. Or maybe I just really want him to catch me.

Either way, he scoops me in via an arm around my waist, bringing me up against the solid length of his body. As always, his touch makes sensation spiral inside me and pool in my nipples and lower belly.

"Hi," he says, eyes glittering in the mellow lighting cast by the lamp on the console. I can't help but notice that his voice is husky now. Can't help but hear the way it softens just for me. "Good to see you. Glad to hear my nickname again."

"Oh, you noticed that?" I say, heart thundering as I tip my face up and let my eyelids drift closed.

"I noticed that."

It takes his kiss a second or two to come, precious time during which my skin heats and anticipation builds. It finally lands on my neck, lingering in the sweet hollow where my shoulder connects and making me hum with pleasure. He pulls back and then, as though he can't help himself, comes in again for a kiss to my forehead.

"Stop trying to seduce me." He takes my hand and leads me deeper into the apartment. "We're trying to get to know each other again. And I've got to get you fed."

"What have you been cooking— Oh, your apartment is *beautiful*."

That's an understatement. His place is a massive fifty-fourth-floor masterpiece of soaring windows and skyline views with the river off in the distance. If it didn't set him back at least ten mil, then I'm Jennifer Lopez in disguise. He's got a gourmet kitchen. A giant TV on the wall. A boxy black leather sofa. Not much else.

"It's not quite home yet," he says, heading for the kitchen. "Just bought it. Haven't had time to call in a decorator yet. Pour yourself some wine. Pour me some, too."

"Sauvignon Blanc," I say, reaching for the bottle chilling in the bucket on the coffee table. "Oh, and it's my favorite label."

"I know. You didn't think I forgot, did you?"

Scoffing at the implication that he'd remember such a minute detail about me after all this time, I glance around to congratulate him on his lucky guess. But then I notice the huge bouquet of blue hydrangeas on the kitchen counter... The platter of black-and-white cookies and the

Magnolia Bakery box… The look in his eyes as he stares straight at my face and into some secret part of me that only he's ever been able to access.

"You didn't think I forgot, did you?" he says again, quieter this time.

Maybe that's the moment that it occurs to me that I'll have to fight a lot harder than this if I want to stop myself from falling more in love with him than ever. That's also when it occurs to me that maybe I don't want to stop myself at all.

"Thank you," I tell him, holding his gaze across the distance.

"My pleasure, Starlight."

We watch each other for a bit longer, until the electricity arcing between us gets hot enough to scorch whatever he's cooking on the stove.

He hastily turns away, grabbing a spoon.

I hastily turn away, my cheeks burning, and pour the wine.

I clear my throat, straining my brain to think of something to say or do that doesn't involve either his bed or me confessing feelings for him that I have no business confessing.

His apartment. We were talking about his *apartment*.

I clear my throat.

"Was this place your little gift to yourself after you went public with your company?" I ask.

"It was."

"No fast car or motorcycle?"

He flashes a wicked smile. "Oh, I got those too."

"Why am I not surprised?" I say, rolling my eyes as I head to the kitchen with our wine.

Easy shrug from Liam. "I keep telling you. Some

things don't change that much."

The comment and his expression are both a little too pointed for me, so I focus on what's in the pot.

"Is that chicken marsala?" I ask, unable to contain my delight.

"Yep. I know it's your favorite. Or used to be. And I'm not dragging my ass to Olive Garden to get you some."

The reference makes me laugh. "Remember the time they threw us out because *you* ate too many breadsticks?"

"You get *endless* breadsticks," he says. "Why would they say that they didn't mean it?"

"Probably because they'd never seen anyone eat them like *you* did," I say, snorting.

"That's on them."

So many memories pass through my mind as we stand there grinning at each other that they create a throb of sweet remembrance. Like the time I woke up with the flu at two a.m. and he ran out to grab juice and soup for me, then held me while I shivered with fever. All the times we studied together at our small kitchen table. Our second and final Christmas together, when we waited too long to look for a tree and wound up with a pitiful Charlie Brown version, which was all they had left at the lot.

A shadow crosses over my heart.

"Is that what we're doing here? Walking down memory lane?"

His stirring slows down. He turns off the burner. Guess he can't cook and hit me with that keen x-ray vision at the same time. Good to know he's a mere mortal in some areas of his life.

"We're walking down memory lane right now, yeah. We're also finishing what we started. We can do both."

It sounds so easy when he says it like that. As though it's eminently possible rather than wishing for the stars.

"Good," I say, passing him his glass of wine and grateful I have something to do other than fall to his feet in gratitude. I seriously need to get a grip on myself and my ever-changing emotions. I can't keep swinging between pending despair and overwhelming euphoria every time the man says something or looks in my direction. If only I knew how to pace myself where he's concerned. "Let's make a toast, then."

"To new beginnings?" he says, raising his glass.

"No," I say, deciding to take what feels like a huge emotional risk for me. Especially when we lock eyes and his gaze threatens to blind me with its intensity. "To my first love."

Liam goes very still, his glass suspended halfway to his lips.

"Who grew up to be exactly the sort of brilliant doctor I knew he'd be the first time I met him," I continue. "And who also looks very sexy in his lab coat. I'm so proud of you, Liam. I was proud when I cyber-stalked you and saw that you'd graduated from med school. And when I cyber-tracked pretty much your entire career. I've been proud of you this whole time. Even if it was from a distance. I just want you to know that. So…to *you*."

Liam keeps still and quiet. Doesn't even blink.

Mia, you big freaking idiot, I think, my heart sinking and bottoming out somewhere in the basement of this high-rise. *You always go one step too far, don't you? You can't just make a standard toast and leave it at —*

Liam springs to life with no warning other than a low rumble of impatience as he sets his drink on the counter without ever sipping it. He yanks my glass from me and sets it down next to his.

Then he reaches for me, and I fall all over him.

This is no tender little kiss. His touch is rough as his hands close on either side of my head. Urgent. His mouth covers mine and latches on, insistent and persuasive. His tongue sweeps deep, but it's not enough for me. It never is when it comes to him. I wrap my arms around his neck and press closer, savoring the gathering tension in his vibrant body and the unmistakable bulge that feels heavy against my belly.

Someone groans. Hell, maybe it's both of us. I can no longer tell where he ends and I begin. His roving hands filter through my hair and rub their way down my back before settling on my ass. His flexing fingers dig into my cheeks, urging me to hop up as he swings me around and plunks me on the counter. I can't open my legs fast enough for him. Can't wrap my thighs tight enough around his waist. Can't breathe with wanting him and wanting to drown in his clean linen scent.

"I *missed* you," he says when he lets me up for air, his voice hoarse. He thrusts against me, his hips hitting my sweet spot and making pleasure spiral with every powerful swivel. "I'm surprised missing you didn't kill me."

"I missed *you*."

His hands massage their way up my thighs and under the hem of my dress, to my panties. I wiggle my way out of them with the speed of Houdini trying to escape a straitjacket before he drowns in a tank of water. Then Liam goes to work on his belt.

"Tell me you still love me." His eyes are right there, blazing with energy. "I need to hear it."

His use of the L-word in this uninhibited moment is like a dropping guillotine separating me from my lust. It's not that I don't want to tell him. It's that it's terrifying how effortless it would be to tell him. I tense and clamp my legs shut to back him up and keep him out, suddenly feeling way too raw and vulnerable. It would be so easy to give him my body and everything else he wants. So easy to sweep any longstanding doubts and fears under the rug and just surrender to this thing that feels inevitable.

But my heart still remembers the burns and the wounds and the abject heartbreak of discovering that he was sleeping with someone else while I was crying over him. The dumb organ never got the memo that that's all ancient history now and we're trying to move on with our lives.

And, judging by the bleakness that edges out the euphoria in Liam's expression, he knows it.

"I'm not ready for that," I say, ducking my head as I pull my skirt down and try not to feel quite so naked. "I'm sorry."

To his credit, he attempts a gracious and understanding smile before pressing a tender kiss to my forehead.

"It's okay. Don't apologize." He rescues my panties from the floor and hands them back to me, never quite looking me in the eye. "We'll get there."

But I turn away as I hop down, slide my panties back on and try to catch my breath and compose myself, not at all sure that we can or will.

16

LIAM

"HOW ARE YOU DOING, DR. WILDER?" says the uniformed doorman at Mia's apartment building one evening about a month later as he lets me inside. "Good night so far?"

"They're all good nights these days," I say, clapping him on the shoulder as I head for the elevator.

My mind shifts to the seamless way that Mia and I have rewoven our lives together over the last few weeks. Calls and texts during the day. Lunch when we can steal the time away from our respective jobs. Evenings spent grabbing dinner or cooking in, at her place and mine, although we've thankfully progressed from our packaged ramen noodle phase. Nights spent whispering and laughing together, snuggled under the blankets with our arms and legs twined and her hair, fragrant and silky, trailing across my bare chest. Full-on sex has stayed firmly on the back burner during the reacquaintance period (although we've done a little cheating around the edges; let's be honest), but I've made my peace with it because I know it's both temporary and for the greater good.

And because tonight will hopefully be the night that I seal this deal, once and for all.

It's Mia for me. Always has been, always will be. Since the second I laid eyes on her.

As for the time we spent apart, it was a painful but needed interruption in our relationship to give us the time we needed to grow up and get our shit together. To learn to appreciate what we have and how we complement each other. Now we're there. Back on track and stronger than ever.

Is it a bit soon for grand gestures? Maybe, but my gut tells me the time is right. So I'm not formulating any backup plans in case she turns me down again. I'm leading with my heart, just like I did before, and keeping the faith that things will work out this time. Why not? We're both in our mid-thirties now. Not exactly one-foot-in-the-grave territory, but we're older. Wiser. And we'd better get a move on if we want a couple of kids before it's too late. Which I desperately do.

At the thought of Mia and me, say, moving to an apartment closer to the park so we can push a baby around in a stroller...watching a little kid clumsily trying to kick a soccer ball around a field...putting everything we've got into the conception process and enjoying every second of it...

I feel a rush of pleasure so intense that it makes the tips of my ears burn.

"No complaints from me," I tell the doorman, feeling sheepish now as he smiles indulgently. "I'm walking on sunshine."

"I see that."

I pause.

"It's Mia's birthday," I add in a conspiratorial tone.

This is how I am these days. So freaking happy with everyone and everything that I can't help but pester random strangers and passing acquaintances with the details. Good thing I don't have kids or a dog. The poor doorman here would be stuck looking at every picture on my phone.

"Oh, yeah? I'm sure you'll do it up nice for her."

"That's the plan," I say, beaming as though this is an audition for a toothpaste commercial. "I've got a few surprises up my sleeve. I want to make it a night we won't forget."

"Have fun."

"We will."

I wave when the elevator arrives. I get in. Obsessively pat my pocket, checking to make sure the small velvet cube is still safely inside. Check my watch to make sure I'm still running on time. Grin at the sappy guy in the mirror.

My phone buzzes just as I step out on her floor. It's Michael, as planned.

"What've you got?" I say, taking care to keep my voice quiet as I start down the hallway.

"You're all set."

"You sure? There's no room for error tonight," I say.

His exasperated sigh comes through loud and clear. "Yeah, I'm sure. You're proposing to my sister, not leading SEAL Team Six on a raid to kill bin Laden. Get a grip. You don't want to give away the surprise."

"That's a ridiculous suggestion. I'm going to need a

handful of Valiums before this is all over. What about the flowers?"

"Check."

"Candles?"

"Check. Just shoot me a text when you're on your way and I'll light them and disappear before you get here. What's your ETA again?"

"Probably close to two hours, by the time we eat dinner and get over there," I say. "I've got a reservation, but you just never know with traffic."

"No worries. That's what I'm here for."

"I owe you. Big time. I would've taken care of it all myself if my surgery hadn't run so long this afternoon."

"You bet your ass you owe me. This is a great place, by the way. She's gonna love it."

"I hope so," I say, succumbing to another round of grinning as I picture the look on her face when she sees my second little surprise of the night. "It's nothing less than she deserves."

"Godspeed. Later."

"Later," I say, laughing.

I tap on her door and try to tamp down some of my rising excitement as I wait for her to answer. We haven't exchanged keys to each other's apartments yet, but hopefully we'll pole-vault over that issue tonight—

"Hey," she says, swinging the door open. And there she is, my own personal burst of sunshine, beaming at me as though I've shown up with a fluffy and beribboned golden retriever puppy tucked under each arm. That's how she greets me every time we see each other these days and, I gotta tell you, I'm addicted. "You're early."

"Had to come see my birthday girl, didn't I?" I sling

an arm around her waist, reel her in and engulf her in a bear hug that leaves only the tips of her toes grazing the floor. She's wearing a silky kimono that slip-slides beneath my hands and emphasizes her supple curves. I linger longer than strictly necessary before letting her go, not gonna lie. But these mini-reunions have become one of the best parts of my day. It's as though I'm in suspended animation when we're apart and come back to life when we're together. "How's your day been? You'd better get dressed, by the way. You're going to make us late for our reservation."

"I know, I know," she says, looking flustered. "I got sidetracked. Something came up."

"Uh-oh. What is it?"

"You grab your drink. I know you need to unwind after your surgery. Meet me in the bedroom. I just need to throw on my dress."

She hurries off, leaving me to do what I do every time I come, which is pour myself a scotch and soda from her liquor cabinet in the corner, sling my jacket over the arm of her sofa and roll up my shirt sleeves, relaxing by degrees. Oh, and she set out a cheese plate. God, I love that woman. She knows I don't always get time for lunch and tries to insert herself between me and hangry whenever possible. I help myself, not realizing until this moment how hungry I am. After a few sips and a couple more crackers, I start to feel human again. She's got Coldplay coming from her high-end speakers—something about paradise; how ironic—and the music also helps break up some of my tension. As long as I keep it low-key and don't get carried away with my excitement, I may be able to give Mia the surprise of a lifetime.

So imagine *my* surprise when I finally wander into the bedroom and see the fully packed suitcase open on her bed.

"What's all this?" I say, my anticipatory smile fading. "Running away?"

"No, silly," she says, hurrying out of the bathroom in another one of her sexy black dresses and presenting me with her back so I can zip her up. "I got the *best* birthday surprise today."

"Oh, yeah?" I say, trying to keep it upbeat and pretending I don't feel a little deflated.

"Yeah. I got a call from my friend Giancarlo in Milan. We interned together and he's started his own house now. We've always stayed in touch. Anyway, he wants me to come to Milan for a meeting the day after tomorrow. He wants to expand into wedding dresses. He wants to give me the label. I'd be creative director."

Holy shit. I feel a huge swell of pride for her accomplishment. I've seen how hard she works. I know how talented she is and how much she loves wedding dresses. This is the sort of thing she's been dreaming of her entire life.

"That's amazing," I say, meaning it from the bottom of my heart. No one deserves this more. "Congratulations. So well earned."

"Thank you! I'm so excited!"

She comes in for a quick congratulatory kiss and hug before heading to the mirror to check her makeup.

Now is not the time for me to shit all over her thrilling news, but I feel like some clarification is in order.

I hesitate, determined to choose my words carefully.

"So…Milan, did you say?"

"Yeah. He's moved his atelier into a great building with much more space. It sounds amazing. I can't wait to see it. Anyway, I just want to hear his offer and see what his plans are. It's a huge honor. An amazing opportunity."

"Absolutely. So…the job is in Milan?"

"Yeah," she says, now primping her hair. "He'd have a creative director, but he'd still be very involved, obviously."

"Obviously."

She finishes with her hair, turns away from the mirror and gets a good look at my face. Which, admittedly, probably looks as though someone died by this point.

"Hang on. I'm not taking the job." She frowns and comes closer. "You didn't think I was taking the job, did you?"

Much as I'd like to laugh with relief and let that be the end of it, I don't feel that reassured. Matter of fact, I don't feel reassured it all.

"You sound like you're taking the job."

"But I'm not," she says with a game attempt at a comforting smile.

"You sound like you want to take the job," I say quietly.

She doesn't answer, but her wilting smile says it all.

And I stand there, frozen.

An idiot Popsicle.

"I'm not leaving New York, Liam. But…I can't lie. It's a dream offer. And I'm really flattered to be considered. If I were at another point in my life, I probably would take the offer."

"You *did* take the offer at another point in your life," I

remind her, my ego stinging from the implication that New York figures into her calculus not to leave, but *I* don't. "I didn't think we'd wind up in the exact same spot again."

"Thanks for throwing that in my face," she says, looking hurt. "I thought we were trying to move on."

"So did I."

We stare at each other, a gulf opening between us. I can almost see the fault lines developing on her hard-wood floor as this domestic earthquake rocks our Richter scale.

I force myself to take a breath and calm down. Today is her birthday. We've got big plans. Great plans. Now is not the time to give my inner asshole free rein, nor is it the moment to let my insecurities come out and play.

But *Christ*. I really didn't think we'd spend tonight talking about the possibility of her leaving me *again*. Especially so soon after we reconnected.

"Look," I say, blowing out a breath as I run my hands over the top of my head and try not to let my frustration get the best of me. I don't want this whole situation to deteriorate. "New York is a fashion capital of the world, right? Is there something about this job that you couldn't, I don't know, do right here?"

"Again: I'm not taking this job, Liam," she says, sounding a lot firmer this time.

I want to be happy about that. I really do. But I'm about to screw up all my battered courage and propose to this woman for a *second* time. My courage only goes so far. I don't have it in me to survive another rejection. I barely recovered the first time.

"Just...humor me," I say.

"I mean..." She hesitates. Whatever it is sitting there on the tip of her tongue, she doesn't want to tell me about it. I know she doesn't. I watch her formulating an answer that she hopes won't hurt my feelings, my tension spiking. "It's Giancarlo. He's offering his name. His brand. His experience. I can't get that here. But I'm *fine* with that. Which is why I'm going to take this meeting in Milan, politely decline and wish him well while also maintaining that connection. Any savvy professional would do the exact same thing, and you know that. Okay? Can we go have my birthday dinner now?"

Well, there it is. My graceful way off this playing field before I get seriously injured and sidelined. All I need to do is grab on to that lifeline, block out my doubts, take Mia out to dinner and execute my plans for tonight.

Simple, right?

Too bad I can't escape this sickening feeling of déjà vu. Once again, it feels like Mia's on a trajectory and I'm on a separate trajectory that has no intersecting points with hers. Once again, it feels like the universe is popping in to rip the rug out from under my feet. Our promising future is about to slam into the side of a cliff and explode on impact. And there's not a damn thing I can do about it.

Just like there was nothing I could do about it when Mia left the first time.

Just like there was nothing I could do about it when our baby stopped growing or when my father dropped dead when I was seventeen.

If there's one lesson I've learned in my life, boy, that's it. Right there in a nutshell.

The people you count on the most can disappear out of your life like *that*.

"*Liam*. Say something."

She's watching me with those big baby blues of hers, looking as scared as I feel. Those eyes have always been the death of me. It would be so easy to push aside my doubts and talk myself into believing her. But then I'd still have an asterisk in my life if I proposed to her tonight, and I'm done with that.

So the proposal's on hold. And I will just have to deal with this renewed sensation of having it all one second and watching it all slip away the next.

It's more important to get this right. And to get it right without anger or ugliness.

"Go to Milan," I say quietly. "Listen to what he has to say. Give it a real chance. Decide what you want to do."

"I don't need to decide, Liam," she says, her voice pitching higher. I watch her with detached curiosity, unable to decide whether she's trying to convince me or herself. "I keep telling you. There's no decision to make."

"Not just about the job. About you and me."

She tenses, a shadow slowly spreading over her expression.

"What do you mean?" she says with unmistakable trepidation.

"I need you to decide. You're either in or you're out."

"That's what we're doing. That's what we've been doing this last month."

I shake my head. I'm done with denials. Done with tiptoeing around this thing. Sure, I'm scared, but so what? That's no reason not to reach for the brass ring.

"That's what *you've* been doing," I say. I feel suddenly liberated, like a tiger allowed to run free for the first time after years of being cooped up in an enclosure. "*I've* decided. I can't keep my feelings for you on lockdown. My heart won't stay in a cage. It wants what it wants when it comes to you, Mia."

For a moment she seems too stunned to respond.

"We've been through some things, Liam," she says, color rising over her cheeks as she presses a hand to her heart. I'm fairly sure I also see the sparkle of tears, which kills me. I'd hoped we'd shed our last tears over each other. Guess I was wrong. "We've hurt each other. Maybe you get over things faster than I do, but I can't just trust you again right this second because you've decided it's time."

"Fair enough," I say. "But I want you to bear something in mind when you're in Milan. Thinking about our future and whether I'm capable of being faithful. You listening?"

"Yep," she says, wiping her eyes.

"I'm not about to cheat on you again. *Ever*. Not when I've spent all this time paying for that one stupid mistake. You're looking at the most committed guy you've ever seen. You know why? Because every woman I've touched since then has been some variation of you. Your smile. Your hair. Your laugh. Your scent."

"Liam—"

"Don't *Liam* me. None of them ever had your eyes, though, and that's my point. I can't make do with imitations. I can't make do with you dipping your toe in the water here and trying to decide whether you want to dive in or not. We're past that."

"So what are you saying?" she asks, and there's that dread again. Amplified.

"I'm saying that I know what I want and what I don't

want," I say, staring her dead in the face to make sure she gets this. "I'm *very* clear on that, thanks. Now it's your turn. *Decide*. Let me know what you want to do and we can have a birthday do-over. Because we've wasted enough time. And it's way past time for us to officially start our lives together."

WHAT THE HELL JUST HAPPENED? How did my lovely birthday evening turn into this junkyard fire fueled by burning rubber and ruined dreams? Can someone kindly explain that to me?

After we cancel our plans and Liam leaves, I collapse onto my sofa in a shell-shocked silence, torn between the temptation to lapse into an epic crying jag and the urgent need to go after him and somehow make things right.

Only I can't move.

I stare blindly at my fireplace mantel, my birthday celebration forgotten. My trip to Milan forgotten. Those things now seem comically insignificant next to my desire to figure out how things went sideways on us so quickly.

Again.

It seems like there should be some warning if my life is about to implode. I should get an opportunity to brace myself. Even a bomb comes with a countdown clock and/or a ticking sound. *Something*. Why can't the universe play fair when it comes to me and Liam? Why can't we have more than ten good minutes together every decade or so?

On the other hand, maybe those aren't the questions at all. Maybe I should ask why I never get smart where he's concerned. And why I persist in thinking/hoping/praying we can finally get our shit together despite all evidence to the contrary.

I'm not sure how long I sit there like that, but eventually some of my paralysis wears off. I ignore my churning belly, reach for my glass of wine and kill it. Feeling marginally better once the alcohol hits my system, I grab Liam's glass and kill that, too. At that point, it just seems wasteful to leave the rest, so I grab the bottle and take a healthy swig or two. Then I slump back against the cushions, curl my feet under me and try to take a good, hard look at my life.

But I'm too wired and scared to think clearly. Worse, my brain only generates two insistent thoughts right now.

What the hell just happened? and *Don't you screw this up, Mia.*

I know I need to take decisive action. Do something to get myself out of this mess.

If only I could figure out *what.*

Should I call Liam? Try to explain that I—

Knock—knock—knock.

I set the bottle down and shoot up like the cola from a two-liter during some middle school science experiment, my heart in my throat as I race for the door.

Liam.

I break into a trot, determined to tell him that nothing on earth means as much to me as he does. To explain things better this time. To work harder on my word choice and do whatever else it takes to bridge the divide that opened between us.

"Liam, I—" I say, swinging the door open.

Only it's not Liam.

It's my brother.

"Michael." My disappointment and disbelief are so overwhelming that I catch myself looking over his shoulder to make sure he's not hiding Liam in the hallway somewhere. I don't bother trying to hide my dismay. I don't have the energy. "What are *you* doing here?"

He scowls as he edges by me, heading straight for the living room. "No, what are *you* doing here? That's the question."

"What?" I ask blankly, shutting the door and following him.

"You had plans. With Liam. Why aren't you doing that?"

"What do you know about my plans with Liam?" I say, startled.

He hesitates as he drops onto the sofa, his expression taking on a distinct *oh, shit, I've said too much* look.

"Don't worry about it. What the hell happened?"

I don't know why I'm surprised that Liam ratted me out to my brother already. Those two always were thick as conjoined thieves. Anyway, it doesn't matter and I'm not planning to look this gift horse in the mouth. I'm just glad he's here to help me debrief the smoldering wreckage of my night. No one dispenses common sense and wisdom like Michael does. And he knows both me and Liam like the back of his hand, so this is perfect.

I can't spill my guts fast enough.

"I don't even know," I say morosely as I settle next to him on the sofa. "I was packing for my trip to Milan—"

"Hang on," he says, stiffening. "You're going to Milan? *Tonight*?"

"No, tomorrow," I say, determined to slow down and take it from the beginning. "I got an offer to be the creative director for a new line of wedding dresses by one of my colleagues from the fashion house I interned at after graduation."

He reels as though I've announced I'm heading to Milan to study organic cannibalism.

"You're moving to Milan after you and Liam just got back together? Jesus Christ, are you trying to ruin the guy once and for all?"

"Of course not!" I cry, equally stung by the accusation and his vehemence. "That's what I tried to tell him!"

"Then why are you going?" he says, now regarding me like I've taken to wearing full clown face makeup in public every day. "What's the point? Other than to freak Liam out and waste the guy in Milan's time?"

"I'm so sorry," I say, outrage getting the best of me. "I didn't realize that *my* thrilling job offer had anything to do with *Liam*. I thought I was networking with a colleague. I thought I was exploring my options and trying to make wise career moves."

Derisive snort from my brother. "You may have been doing all that, but why are you leaving out the big thing you're doing? The main thing?"

"And what's that?" I say acidly.

"Making sure you have an escape hatch with Liam," he says, taking his emotional nail gun and using it to hit me right between the eyes. "Making sure you have one foot firmly planted out the door at all times so you don't get hurt if things don't work out."

I cringe.

I hesitate.

I finally crank my mouth open, only to realize, after an embarrassing delay, that I have no credible comeback.

Possibly because he's right, not that I'm ready to admit it. Not when my brain is still scanning his analysis through my internal truth-o-meter and my cheeks have suddenly caught fire.

"I don't know what you're talking about," I say, aiming for dignified disdain and failing hopelessly. "I don't think that's true at all."

"It *is* true. What's going on here?" He hits me with that piercing gaze of his, the one that makes it hard to think and impossible to hide. "Do you want things to work out with him or not?"

This time there's no hesitation. My heart is too full of Liam to bother denying it.

"Of course I do!"

Something in his expression softens. Maybe there's even a hint of understanding.

"What gives, Mia?" he says, his voice gentler now.

I open my mouth, and out pops a bunch of stuff I didn't even know was still lurking in there.

"I'm so scared," I say, rubbing my aching chest. If only I knew a good heart surgeon who could come and make sure mine is in good working order. Oh, that's right. I do. Only I drove him off earlier, didn't I? "It's like I don't believe in love anymore. Like that part of me is broken or shut down or something."

"Good point. Too bad we don't know anyone who's been successful at relationships. Someone who could set a good example. Oh, wait. We do. Mom and Dad. Who've been married for *forty years*."

"What have *they* got to do with *me*?" I say with simmering frustration. "To my knowledge, Dad never slept with someone else who then called Mom to tell her about it in excruciating detail."

He grimaces. "That was bad. No argument there."

"Gee, thanks."

"But if you want to be with this guy, there has to come a point where you decide to let it go and move on. At some point, you have to make a leap of faith. You either decide he's worth it, or he's not. Simple."

"Well, *thank you* for mansplaining all that to me. Why on earth didn't I turn to you sooner?"

"I could do without the sarcasm," he says, scowling. "I'm trying to help you here."

"When is the actual help going to come?"

"Right now," he says, resting his elbows on his knees and leaning in. "You wouldn't know this because you were busy traipsing around Milan at the time—"

"I wasn't *traipsing*," I say, incensed by the injustice of this accusation. As if I went on my merry way without a backward glance and had the time of my life, leaving Liam to wallow in the slop of his own misery. "It wasn't all kittens, rainbows and bonbons for me, either."

"Yeah, well, he fell apart. You know that, right?"

The sudden grimness of his expression takes some of the wind out of my sails. I shift uncomfortably.

"What you mean?" I say, not at all sure I want to hear this. Liam mentioned he went through a hard time, yeah, but I get the sudden unwelcome feeling that he didn't tell me the half of it.

"I mean he didn't eat. He lost a good twenty pounds.

Didn't sleep. Partied his ass off. There was a period there when the rest of the guys and I kept an eye on him. We weren't sure what he would do."

The silent implication turns my blood to ice.

"He didn't — ?" I say.

"No. Thank God." He gives me a pointed look. "I'm telling you that some guys are cheaters. They never learn from their mistakes. They'll never be faithful. No one should expect them to. I have friends like that. Hell, I thought Liam was like that early on. But then he met *you*."

Right on cue, the ice begins melting inside me. As though someone flipped a switch deep in some hidden recess of my body that I wasn't aware I had. I begin to breathe easier. I begin to hope about the future in a way I hadn't until this very second.

Of all the people in the world, my brother will never lie to me. He has no agenda other than wanting me to be happy. I trust him to Jupiter's outer moons and back.

"How can I get past this fear?" I ask. "I'm tired of being stuck. I want to be sure."

"Do you love him? Don't think. Just answer from the heart. Yes or no?"

"Yes," I say, surprised by how easily the answer flows once I stop trying to block it. *"Yes."*

"Then you're sure," he says, shrugging. "Easy."

"Yeah, but are *you* sure about my sureness?" I say, trying to manage a powerful surge of euphoria.

He leans even closer. Takes my hands in his. Squeezes them.

"Look into my eyes," he says.

I don't want to — I'm not at all sure I won't burst into tears of one sort or another — but I do.

"Mia. I'm sure."

His eyes radiate compassion and understanding.

A thousand percent.

And I'm so relieved that it's a wonder my soaring joy doesn't lift me off this sofa and fly away with me.

"I hope Liam knows you're sticking your neck way out to vouch for him," I say, grinning.

"He knows he's going to get his ass kicked if he hurts my sister again," he says grimly.

I'm strangely cheered and reassured by the thought. "Threats of violence work for me."

"I thought they might."

"Thanks, Michael," I say, wiping away a happy tear or two.

"Anything for you." He lets go of my hands and palms my face, bringing me in for a peck on the cheek. "Any time."

"Well, not *any* time," I say. "You could've told me all this years ago."

"Maybe," he says, shrugging. "But you wouldn't have listened. You weren't ready. Were you?"

"Oh, whatever." He's teetering dangerously close to smugness now, so I whack him in the belly with the back of my hand. "This *one* time you may have stumbled onto some relevant and wise information by accident, but I'm sure you'll go back to being an idiot tomorrow."

"Sadly true," he says, chuckling.

"What's gotten into you? What gives you the right to be this optimistic about love? You're just coming off a divorce. *I* should be talking *you* down from the ledge."

"Go figure, right?" His attention drifts down to his hands as he absently rubs them. "Actually, my situation is different. It's not like I had it all and let it slip away. I was married to the wrong woman."

That catches my attention.

"What? You've always acted like the two of you just grew apart. I've never heard you say anything like that before."

"Yeah," he says ruefully, rubbing his chin. "I ignored a few doubts before the wedding."

"Now you need to find the right woman."

"I'll have to see what I can do," he says lightly.

A little *too* lightly.

I take a closer look at him and notice the sudden flush concentrating in his high cheekbones.

"Hang on," I say, not bothering to hide my wicked glee. "You've seen the woman you had your eye on when you were married, haven't you? Don't deny it."

"I neither confirm nor deny that allegation."

"Bullshit. At least tell me who she is."

He pauses, looking wistful. "Someone special," he says. "And I'm done with this conversation. We're working on you and Liam tonight. So grab your bag."

"What? Why?"

"You'll see. Let's go. No questions."

The fresh early evening air does me some good, as does the bustle and the twinkling city lights. There's nothing like the Upper East Side on a summer's night. We set out. A ten-minute walk and a couple of lovely tree-lined blocks later, he leads me up the stairs of a gorgeous five-story brownstone with a discreet SOLD sign out front. It's nicely nestled on a street full of upscale boutiques.

"Whose house is this?" I ask, the strangest feeling prickling across my nape.

"I told you. No questions," he says, whipping out a set of keys and unlocking the massive front door.

He ushers me inside, where the doleful strains of Miles Davis feeling kind of blue immediately hit our ears. We skirt the carved staircase to our left and follow the beacon light coming from a set of double doors at the end of the long hallway. He stops on the threshold. Then, without a word, he reaches for my arm and pulls me in front of him so I can see into the room.

I'm not exactly in the mood for a birthday party, but I work on my surprised face in case my friends threw something together for me. So imagine my actual surprise when an altogether different scene greets me.

A magical room alight with the flickering from dozens of pillar candles arranged on windowsills, the mantel and the perimeter. Blue hydrangeas everywhere. A small table laden with chocolate-covered strawberries and a bucket of champagne. A cozy lover's nest in the corner, with cushions and pillows arranged on top of a blanket on the floor.

And in the middle of it all?

Liam slumped in one of the chairs at the table with his elbows on his knees and his head in his hands. I stare at him, my heart shattering into a million pieces because I never meant to do this to him. I've never seen such an image of quiet despair. And if I have my way, I'll never see it again after tonight.

"You gonna put this poor fool out of his misery?" my brother whispers.

"Yes," I say, so overwhelmed with a sudden feeling of gratitude for him that I pull him in for a quick bear hug. *"Thank you."*

"You can thank me by never putting me in the position of knowing this much about your personal business again," he says gruffly when I finally release him. "Now go get your guy."

And he takes off, leaving me to overcome my raging case of nerves and make things right with Liam.

18

LIAM

I BLEW IT.

Actually, I blew it twice, didn't I? First by giving Mia that ridiculous and misguided ultimatum or whatever it was earlier. Then I re-blew it by coming *here* to lick my wounds rather than going home to drink myself into oblivion like a normal person would. It's like I wanted to rub my own idiot face in the candles and all this other shit from the proposal that wasn't. Like I needed to maximize the misery.

Now here I am. King of Fools.

I rub my hands over my face and drop into one of the chairs, doing my best not to choke on my frustration.

I don't know *what* that was. I don't know where the words came from. I don't know who told me to say it. Swear to God, I don't. All I know is that I felt like I was doing the right thing when I told her to decide what she wants. Like I had divine guidance when I took that ridiculous stand. Now I feel abandoned and moronic. God or the universe or whoever has clammed up when it comes to dispensing advice. And I'm positive I shot myself in the foot with a twelve-gauge shotgun for no good reason.

Why couldn't I wait? Why couldn't I be patient? She said she was just going to network and maintain a valuable connection. Why didn't I believe her? Why couldn't I let events unfold at their own pace and trust our relationship?

Why do I have to be an idiot at every opportunity?

Why can't I let an idiot opportunity pass every now and then? Wouldn't *that* make sense?

So…

What now, Romeo?

Blowing out a breath, I bend at the waist, put my elbows on my knees and plant my face in my hands.

What now?

Go back to her place and apologize?

Grab flowers before going back to her place to apologize?

Or…

Should I stick to my guns now that we've started down this path?

Yeah, says a distant voice in my head. *Stick to your guns*.

Without warning, I get an unsettling flash of my father.

Hard as it is to believe, he was just a few years older than I am now when he dropped dead from cardiac arrest. I'm sure he thought he had more time. But he crammed a lot into the life he lived. More than I have, for sure. He was married. It was a shit marriage, true, but he and my mother loved each other at one point. They had me, so he had a family well before he hit my age. Hell, he had *two* families if you include his mistress and Ella. His mistress was the love of his life, by all accounts. And he spent years playing house with her while remaining in a toxic marriage with my mother. And for what? So he could drop dead before he ever grew the balls to go after what he wanted?

I don't want that to be me. I don't know much, but I know *that*. Life is short. Mia and I have already wasted over a decade with bullshit even though I knew when I met her that lightning had just struck my life. It's time for us to be together and build that family we almost started. And if I need to stow away in her luggage and move to Milan to do that, I'm more than happy to.

Stick to your guns, that voice says again.

Great. Now I have a plan. If I could just figure out how to —

"Liam. Hey."

I snap to attention and sit up straight at the sound of Mia's voice cutting across Miles Davis, my pulse rate kicking into maximum overdrive. Her sudden appearance is so startling that she might have been a ghost conjured from midair. Or maybe a fantasy spun to life by my overactive imagination. She lingers in the doorway, her expression indecipherable as I drop my hands and try to get my shit together.

"Hey," I say, reaching for my phone and turning the music down.

"Didn't mean to startle you."

"It's okay."

"My brother brought me."

"I figured."

There's a pause.

"He had a few stern words for me," she says ruefully.

I don't want or need to know the specifics. Michael

would never betray any of my confidences. And he genuinely wants happiness for both of us. I know he does.

"Ah. Do I need to kill him or thank him?"

"Remains to be seen," she says.

Another pause. We stare at each other across the space of about twenty feet while my heart wedges itself tight into my throat. She opens her mouth and hesitates, clearly gearing up for some big speech. I'm tempted to let her off the hook and tell her not to bother. Part of me wants to reassure her that nothing else matters as long as she's here now. No explanations necessary. I'll wait another twelve years for her if I need to. But that inner voice is yammering in my ear again, louder now.

Stick to your guns.

"Mind if I come in?" she asks.

"Please."

She comes closer, giving the scene an appreciative once-over. "This is beautiful. Really beautiful."

"Glad you like it. I'm just hoping no one calls the fire marshal on me."

She grins, breaking through some of the awkwardness and setting off a series of cartwheels and flips deep in my gut.

"I'm getting the feeling I'm missing a great birthday."

"You're missing a fantastic birthday," I say.

"I'd like to have my do-over now," she says quietly as she comes to stand by the table. "If it's not too late."

My throat loosens up enough for me to breathe again.

"It's never too late, Starlight."

"Good," she says, flashing a relieved smile. "I was afraid I blew it."

"I was afraid *I* blew it. I want you to be happy. If

you're happy, *I'm* happy. If you need Milan to be happy, then let's start packing. They probably have a hospital or two in Milan that needs a good heart surgeon. I just need to know that I'm part of your future."

"What about the fact that I'm still crazy in love with you?" she says, unsmiling, as she runs her fingers through the hair at my temple and makes me shiver. "Do you need to know that?"

My heart stops. Absolutely ceases all function, leaving me to fend for myself.

"That's pertinent information, yeah," I say hoarsely.

She hits me with the steady beam of those amazing blue eyes, a force so bright and powerful that it's a wonder I'm not immediately blinded.

"I'm crazy in love with you, Liam. Consider yourself informed."

"I'm crazy in love with *you*." It's also a wonder that my voice works at all right now, when I'm so overcome with emotion that a catastrophic system failure seems inevitable. "Just so *you* know."

"That's really good to hear," she says, laughing. Then, to my astonishment, she reaches into her pocket and produces her engagement ring. The sight of that glittering diamond shining on her palm does crazy things to me, I gotta tell you. As does the subtle hint of mischief in her expression now. "While we're clearing things up, I thought I'd bring this back to you. I've been carrying it around, but I wouldn't want something so precious to get lost on my watch."

"Good thinking," I say gravely, deciding to play along. "Or you could just keep it. You're a responsible person."

"Yeah." She frowns down at it still in her hand. "Where should I keep it? Back in my pocket?"

"Gosh. I don't know. Seems like it might be more secure on one of your fingers."

"Hmmm," she says, repressing a smile with difficulty. "Which one?"

"Let's see which one it fits."

I take the ring, glance up at her face—she seems to be holding her breath and close to bursting with excitement—and reach for her right hand.

"Liam Wilder!" she squawks, snatching her hand away. "Don't even try it!"

I would laugh at her outrage, but the moment suddenly seems far too momentous for that. I've dreamed of this moment. Lived for it. Feared it would never come again.

Without a word, I take her trembling left hand and slide it onto her ring finger.

"It still fits," she says, admiring it on her hand. "Oh my God."

It's a pretty little ring. The best my budget could afford at the time, way back when I couldn't access the money in my trust and had to make do as a standard college student.

But I can do better now.

"I don't like it," I say, sliding it off again and ignoring her indistinct sound of protest. "This is a bad idea."

Her entire body wilts.

"Liam..."

She looks so wounded, poor thing. And I don't have the heart to do this to her.

So I quickly drop out of the chair and to my knee, reaching for the little velvet box in my pocket at the same time. By the time I get the box open, her disappointment has given way to wide-eyed astonishment. Then she gets a look at the flawless and sparkly ten-carat emerald-cut diamond and her jaw drops.

"Please." I meant to make a whole speech here about how much she means to me and how I swear I'll take good care of her for the rest of our lives. Give her the earth because she makes me so happy. But now that the moment is here, I'm so overcome with emotion that I can barely get the words out. "Be my wife."

"Oh my God," she cries, her attention going back and forth between my face and the ring, which is pretty damn fabulous if I say so myself. "Yes!"

"Yes?"

"*Yes!*"

That's all I need to hear. I slide the baby on her finger, where I knew it belonged the second I saw it out of all the rings I looked at, toss the box aside and rise to my feet.

Urgency consumes me as I reach for her, my dick surging to complete hardness as though it's been launched from a catapult. It's been a month since I was inside her, and that's way too long. Urgency consumes her, too, judging by the way she welcomes me with open arms and sultry laughter. I ride a wave of euphoria as I take her face in my hands and kiss her forehead and her long-lashed eyes, her cheeks and the scattered freckles across her cheeks. Then I make my way to her lush mouth, already half out of my mind from the feeling of her plump berry lips and the voluptuous sweep of her tongue.

One of us groans. One of us gasps. Who the hell knows at this point? We can't hold each other tight enough. We can't undress each other fast enough. I back her toward the nest of pillows in the corner, her eager hands helping me shrug out of my jacket. It hits the floor. I toe my way out of my shoes, our mouths still fused. She kicks off her heels and reaches for my tie, working hard to loosen it. Much as I appreciate the effort, we have the rest of the night and, better yet, the rest of our lives to get fully naked. And we don't need my bare chest for what I have in mind for her right now.

"Forget it," I say, gasping as I come up for air and reach for the hem of her dress. "We've got bigger fish to fry."

My fiancée flashes a wicked grin. "Good point."

We jointly sweep her dress over her head and toss it aside. I marvel at the glowing flesh and the way all that silky black hair swings back into place around her shoulders. To my immense pleasure, there's no bra tonight. Just the engorged pink nipples dotting the gentle swells of her breasts. My greedy hands help themselves to her bare skin as we tumble down to the cushions, reveling in her warmth and supple strength as she arches against me.

Though I want to encourage her to wrap those toned thighs tight around my waist so I can grind against her right now, it occurs to me that there's a better way to go about this. So I shift to one side, opening enough space for the two of us to undo my belt, unzip my fly and grab my dick.

I need to be inside her. *Need* it.

But I also need to take a moment to savor this glorious view because she's heavy-lidded. Flushed. Breathless.

Mine for the taking. Absolutely astonishing.

I shake my head at myself, undone in this overheated moment.

"I love you," I say, my voice husky. *"Love. You."*

"And I love *you*," she says, straining to kiss me again and thrusting her hips at the same time.

I can resist a lot of things, but her tongue and her pussy are not on that list, especially when they're both on offer. I grip my dick and drive it home, deep into her slick heat. Birth control never crosses my mind, and I doubt it crosses hers. Her secret muscles clamp tight around me with a grip that has the room fading out of focus.

The things she does to me. Sometimes they stop my breath.

I break the kiss just long enough to get some air into my lungs and make a quick clarification.

"Fuck," I say, urging her to wrap those legs around my waist. "You just signed up for a lifetime of this. You know that, right?"

Another sultry laugh. "Thank God."

Now that we're fully on the same page, I settle in to enjoy and inflame her, picking up the same rhythm with my tongue and my hips and going hard and deep with both. She meets me thrust for thrust, whispering broken bits of words that may have my name swirled in there somewhere. I revel in her skin. Her hair. Her mouth. Her hot pussy.

Fuck. Her *pussy*.

I'd love to claim that, stallion that I am, I made it last all night. I didn't. The best I can say is that I held up long enough for her to come first and, judging by the way she jackknifes and the pitch and velocity of her astonished cry, make it reasonably enjoyable. I stiffen and hurtle off the edge right after her, shuddering and soaring into oblivion with a rapturous smile on my face and love in my heart. I'm exactly that sappy, just that quick.

I roll onto my back when it's over, keeping her right there with me as we form our boneless tangle of limbs. She rests her head on my chest and sighs deeply, a feminine sound of relaxation and satisfaction that stirs me to my core.

"So…" I say, idly twirling a strand of her hair around my finger. "Do I need to start learning Italian?"

"No, silly," she says. "I told you. I'm not moving to Milan. I'm staying right here with you."

"What about your career? What about wedding dresses?"

"I'll figure something out," she says, and I can hear the sleep in her voice. "As long as we're together. By the way, this is a *huge* house you've got here."

"You like it?" I say, now tracing figure eights on her back.

"I love it. The light in here must be amazing during the day. But we don't need this much space. How many kids do you think we're having?"

"It's not a residence," I say, working hard to keep my expression bland. Not that she can see it right now. "It's an atelier. Or it will be."

Her entire body tenses against mine. Her head pops up, revealing wide eyes with the whites visible all around.

"It's a *what*?"

"An atelier." I smother my grin. "It's a French word for a place where you—"

"I know what an atelier is, thanks," she says, smacking my abs. "Whose atelier is it going to be?"

can't be certain, but I think she's holding her
.th.

"It's yours. *Atelier Mia Nova*." I frown thoughtfully. "Unless you know of some other worthy wedding dress designer I should hook up with."

"Nope," she says, laughing and teary now. "I'm the only one for you. I thought you understood that by now."

"I *do* understand that," I say, pulling her in for another kiss. "I understand that perfectly."

∼

Keep reading for a special sneak peak at the first standalone in my **Fairy Tale Billionaires** series (just in case you missed it!), Damon & Carly's story, *The Billionaire's Princess*...

EXCERPT FROM THE BILLIONAIRE'S PRINCESS

She glides in like the queen of everything without bothering to notice the fancy Friday night crowd here at Bemelmans in the Carlyle Hotel on the Upper East Side. Forget about making eye contact with anyone or acknowledging the pianist plinking away on the grand. The server gets a nod of thanks as he seats her at the leather banquette against the wall at one of the small round tables nearest where my brothers and I sit. A hint of a dimpled smile as she accepts the menu. Then the server walks off and she lowers her eyes to study the drink selections, retreating into a cool bubble of aloofness that only the brave would dare try to penetrate.

I am nothing if not brave.

Don't get me wrong. *Brave* is probably not the first word people use to describe me. *Ruthless* comes to mind. As do *arrogant, brilliant* and *rich*. Generally followed by the word *bastard*.

For example? *Damon Black is an arrogant bastard.*

Not that I care what anyone thinks of me. You don't bring your late father's floundering property development company back from the brink of disaster and turn it into a billion-dollar-ish real estate empire by the age of thirty-four by tiptoeing around people's feelings.

But *her*…

I notice everything about her, oblivious to my brothers' ongoing conversation and too riveted to bother lowering my dirty martini all the way back to the table.

The pale skin and vivid auburn hair that seem to distill and concentrate the room's rosy glow on her sleek face and swelling cleavage. The way the spaghetti straps of her little black dress skim her kissable shoulders. The graceful neck and the way a single gleaming corkscrew strand of hair escapes her severe bun and trails down her back. The way her long and shapely legs culminate in pretty feet that feature pink-tipped toes strapped into killer heels.

No rings on her left hand. A funny detail I usually don't care to notice one way or the other but that now gives me a surge of satisfaction that I plan to pretend I don't feel.

She studies the menu. I study her, my skin prickling with awareness as I experience the slow curl of desire in my belly and lower.

"Damon?"

The thing is, this is new for me. Not noticing women in bars, obviously. I notice women. I hook up with women. But lately I do both with all the enthusiasm of a man brushing his teeth before bed. My body needs it and it's got to get done. I may as well get it over with as quickly as possible so I can move on to more important things. My boredom, which teeters on complete indifference most of the time now, is a hazard of the singles scene here in the city as much as my chronic workaholism. I'm not excited by too much of anything these days, except for the huge deal my brothers and I closed this afternoon.

Wanting someone to screw is not new for me.

Wanting anyone the way I suddenly want ye olde ice princess over there? Brand new for me.

I don't believe in romantic love. Let's put that out there right now. My parents blasted the idea out of my head and left a crater for my heart when they savaged each other during their divorce back when I was ten. I jeer at friends who fall "in love." But a woman like *that*? I can understand how she'd put a crazy thought or two into an unsuspecting guy's head.

"Damon? You with us?" one of my brothers asks.

"Shut the hell up," I say mildly without ever looking away from her, ignoring their round of sniggering at my expense as best I can.

The server delivers the woman's martini and slips away again. She looks up suddenly, possibly feeling the weight—or maybe the heat—from all my focused attention on her face. She looks across at me, and our gazes connect. I freeze and do my best to overcome the sensation of landing flat on my ass and having the wind knocked out of me.

She's insanely gorgeous. Huge eyes with sweeping brows. Oval face. The kind of plump berry mouth that'll make a plastic surgeon rich quick around these parts.

I watch as she freezes like I just did. As her mouth opens into a surprised little O. As a telltale blush originates across the tops of her breasts, creeps north and settles in her high cheeks. As her expression cycles through surprise and subtle feminine appreciation before ending in an unmistakable flare of annoyance that makes her lips thin.

My glass continues to hover somewhere near my mouth, so I raise it to her in a toast and die a thousand tiny deaths while I wait for her reaction.

She hesitates, clearly thinking it over. Then, to my utter astonishment, she flashes the beginnings of a sexy smile that promises heaven on earth between her legs. My heart pounds and pounds harder as she stands and shimmies her clingy dress into place with some delightful hip action. My mouth waters, I admit, and keeps watering when she picks up her drink and takes a couple of steps in my direction. My floundering brain recovers enough to order me to stand and greet her, which I start to do. I should mention that I usually prefer to do the hunting, but this works for me. If you're out deep-sea fishing and a swordfish flops onto your boat and lands at your feet, you don't throw the thing back, do you? No. You don't. I'm also usually low-key about these interactions, but there's no stopping my thrilled grin from its complete facial takeover.

Until she stops on the other side of her own little table, lobs a withering frown in my direction and sits facing the banquette she just vacated, presenting me with her lovely back. Leaving me stunned and seriously disappointed.

Like a fucking loser.

My brothers guffaw while I linger there, half up and half down.

"That one's going to leave a nasty bruise in the morning." Griffin, my thirty-two-year-old middle brother, claps me on the back in a mock show of sympathy.

"You're going to want to ice it down before you go to bed *by yourself* tonight."

He's right. I snort back an involuntary laugh as I sit again, rubbing my aching chest under the guise of straightening my tie.

I feel dazed. No shit.

She got me. I'm man enough to admit that. She's got beauty and a sharp sense of humor. I like that. A lot. I'm also betting that she can run pretty hot for the right man.

I *am* that man. I *will* be that man. Tonight, if I can help it.

She can sit there with her back to me all she wants, sipping her martini while congratulating herself on her cleverness. Let her enjoy her brief victory. The poor thing doesn't know that she just took my smoldering fire for her and poured a million gallons of gasoline on it.

But she'll learn.

"Want me to show you how it's done?" says my thirty-year-old youngest brother, Ryker, jerking his head in her direction and starting to stand. Just like that, a haze of red filters my vision, and it has nothing to do with the ambience here at Bemelmans.

"Sure," I say, reaching up to push him back down again with all the force I can muster. "As long as you're cool with that being your last act on earth."

This kicks off another round of raucous laughter between Tweedledee and Tweedledum, but a bigger problem materializes in the form of a corporate titan wannabe who sidles up to her table with his cheesy grin firmly in place. I watch and wait to see how she greets him, the tinge of jealousy I just felt with my brother now escalating into a wave of bloodlust.

It's probably her date. A woman who looks like *that* doesn't spend her Friday nights alone.

But she stiffens when he steps into her range of vision. Shakes her head when he leans in and says something to her. Speaks loudly and clearly when he persists:

"Fuck off."

I register the throaty sound of her voice and the British accent even as my inner caveman takes the lead and propels me to my feet. Pretty ironic, considering I would've sworn as recently as ten seconds ago that I'm not the jealous type.

A murmur of dissent rises from my brothers as I head in her direction without another word.

"Keep it cool," Ryker calls after me. "We'd rather not have to bail you out of jail tonight."

But I'm on a mission and don't have the time or inclination to reassure him. I'm not sitting idly by while some SOB in a shiny suit harasses my ice princess right in front of me. Can't do it.

"Sorry I'm late," I say, putting a protective arm around the back of her chair and startling them both. Shiny Suit shoots me a glare, but I only have eyes for her and the flare of relief in her expression as she tips her face up to look at me. "Everything okay over here?"

If you enjoyed this excerpt, read *The Billionaire's Princess* now!

ALSO BY AVA RYAN

Fairy Tale Billionaires Series

The Billionaire's Princess

The Billionaire's Beauty

The Billionaire's Cinderella

Manhattan Billionaires

His Lost Love

To DH
XOXO

ACKNOWLEDGMENTS

Once again, special thanks to Nina Grinstead and the team at Grey's Promotions for helping me launch this book and to Croco Designs for the lovely covers. And huge thanks to my writer's brain trust of friends. Love you!

Excerpt from *The Billionaire's Princess* © 2020 by Ava Ryan

ABOUT THE AUTHOR

Ava Ryan is an author of sexy contemporary romance. Her favorite things, in no special order, are animals, her family, cookies, people with great senses of humor and love stories. Currently in her writer's cave (ostensibly working hard on her next book while also checking Netflix every few hours to make sure she hasn't missed a new true crime documentary show), she loves hearing from readers via her website or social media.

If you love billionaire alpha males, the feisty women who snag their hearts and books that end with a happily ever after, you've come to the right place.

Please make sure to Subscribe to Ava's VIP List to stay in the loop about her latest releases and upcoming books.

Finally, don't forget to follow her on Amazon and/or BookBub to learn about any special promotions on her books.

Made in the USA
Las Vegas, NV
23 December 2020